ISA & THE DEAL

(THE SUNNYVALE MYSTERIES, BOOK 3)

JESSICA SORENSEN

❀ Created with Vellum

1

ISABELLA

It's been only minutes since Lynn told me Bella—my real mom—was a terrible person who's rotting in her grave. Only a few tiny minutes, yet it feels like an eternity, as if I've entered a time portal where time moves at half-speed.

It gives me too much time to think about my mom being dead, about how angry my dad was that I asked about her, about Lynn and how I shoved her after she told me. I ran out of my house right after without waiting to see her reaction. I was completely hysterical. But thank the damn stars Kai found me; otherwise, who knows what I would've done. In the state of mind I was in, I wanted nothing more than to make the pain go away and would've done almost anything to make it stop.

But by some miraculous miracle—seriously, the guy is

some kind of genius distraction wizard—Kai manages to calm me down. He takes me into the den of his house, tells me to sit down on the sofa, and puts on *Zombieland*. Then he gives me a bowl of popcorn and a box of Milk Duds and lies down on the floor.

I haven't explained to Kai what happened, at least not all the details, but I can tell he's wondering by the way he keeps staring at me instead of watching the movie. It's a zombie movie. No one is that distracted during a zombie movie unless they're deeply thinking about something. Or they're a total weirdo.

"I don't know what to do," I mumble through a yawn when the movie credits appear on the television screen. I roll onto my side to look down at Kai. His light blond hair is flattened on one side, and his cheek is red from where his face was pressed against the pillow. "I'm not sure if I can go home or if I can even call it home. After I pushed Lynn..." I shake my head. "I don't even feel bad. What kind of person does that make me?"

He rotates onto his back and cocks a brow at me. "You pushed Lynn? When?"

"Right after she told me about my mom." Reality crashes down on me. "I'm in so much shit, Kai. My dad was already super pissed I tried to find out about my real mom. He probably already changed the locks so I can't get into the house."

Kai nibbles on his bottom lip, contemplating. "Maybe

that's a good thing. No more Hannah. No more Lynn. You'd finally be free of them."

"Yeah, I know." I twist onto my back, sweeping strands of my brown hair out of my tear-stained face. I'm sure I'm rockin' some awesome raccoon eyes right now and probably look like a real hot mess. Thankfully, it's just Kai here with me. After he apologized to me for what happened in seventh grade, and then I found out about how he told everyone that Hannah lied about me being in a mental institution, I know I can trust him. "I know this is going to sound crazy—it sounds crazy even in my own head—but part of me doesn't want to get kicked out."

When he doesn't respond, I slant to the side to look at him.

He's gaping at me like I just flew over the cuckoo's nest. "I'm going to chalk up your temporary insanity to the fact that you've been through a ton of shit in the last couple of hours and give you a piece of advice. If you can get out of that house, then do it. You'll be better off on your own than living with your psychotic, abusive family."

"They don't abuse me. Yeah, they're mean as hell, but they never hit me or anything like that."

Kai carries my gaze. "Isa, words can sometimes be just as harmful as actions."

I swallow the lump in my throat as I recollect how many times Hannah and Lynn have insulted me. How my dad ignored it. How crappy I felt, how small, how worth-less. Then I think of Kai and how his dad treats him.

"You should take your own advice," I say with an insinuating look.

He shrugs indifferently. "I'm working on it."

I massage my aching chest with my hand, wishing I could get the tightness out. "I wouldn't be on my own if I moved out. I'd move in with my grandma Stephy."

"Good. From what you've told me about her, she sounds pretty cool." He sits up and stretches his arms above his head, causing his black T-shirt to ride up just enough that I get a brief glimpse of his abs.

I try not to gawk like some band groupie ogling a lead singer, but my gaze has other ideas. I blame it on my hormones. When they take over, I lose my self-control.

"Yeah, she's cool..." *Stop staring at him, Isa. You're such a weirdo.* "She's actually the grandma I went on that trip with this summer." I finally manage to tear my gaze off Kai's lean muscles and give myself a mental high-five for regaining my self-control. But then I cringe when I find him watching me with curiosity written all over his face.

He so just busted me.

I trap my next breath in my lungs, waiting for him to tease me, but strangely, he remains quiet. Maybe he's giving me a get-out-of-jail-free pass because he feels sorry for me. While I'm not a huge fan of pity, I'll take the pass.

"It'd still suck to move, though." I say. "I'd have to change schools… I know I don't have a ton of friends or anything, but I was just starting to fall into a good rhythm."

He frowns. "Why would you have to change schools? I thought she lived in Sunnyvale."

"She does but on the other side of town at Sunnyvale Bay Community, which is a different school district." I sit up and lower my feet onto the floor. "It's a thirty-minute drive away from our school, so I'd have to transfer."

He props his elbows on the edge of the sofa only inches away from my legs. "It'll only take thirty minutes if you drive like a grandma."

"My grandma would have to drive me," I point out. "And I don't want to ask her to do that. And even if I did, I don't think she can. She lets Indigo borrow her car for work and stuff. It'd be way easier on everyone if I just transferred." I sigh, tucking my hands underneath my legs. "I just wish I wasn't so socially incompetent."

"You're not socially incompetent. You're just shy."

"Shy, socially incompetent, it still means I have a hard time talkin' to people." I flop back on the sofa. "I wish I could get over it, but I think I'll always be this way."

"Being shy isn't a bad thing." He reaches out to touch me but then pulls back. "And we can get you over it."

"Not everyone can be a beautiful social butterfly like you," I smile for probably the first time since the madness opened up beneath me and tried to swallow me whole. "You're like a unicorn, dude."

His forehead creases. "A unicorn?"

I nod, patting his head. "All rare and majestic. Heads turn when you walk into the room because you're so pretty, and everyone wishes they could be as pretty as you."

He beams at me. "I am pretty amazing."

Yep. There's no use trying to deny Kai's gorgeous. He knows it. All the girls who go to my high school know it. Unicorn lovers everywhere know it.

His grin broadens as he pushes to his feet and plops down on the cushion beside me. "I have an idea."

I dramatically roll my eyes. "Oh, no … Here we go."

He presses his hand to his chest, pretending to be offended. "Hey, not all of my ideas are bad."

I snort a laugh. "Remember that one time you thought it'd be super awesome if I sat on your lap in that rusty swing set because there was only one seat and you wanted me to swing with you?" It was back in seventh grade during our fleeting friendship. When I think back to that time, I did a lot of risky things thanks to Kai. For some reason, I had a hard time saying no to him even when his ideas screamed, *"Danger! Danger! You just might die!"*

He pulls a guilty face. "Yeah, that might not have been my best idea."

"*Might not have been.*" I gape at him. "The damn thing broke when we were in mid-air. I almost broke my arm and crushed your manly parts."

He winces, his hand drifting to his lap. "Yeah, I remember that part too clearly." He considers something before twisting to face me. "What if I promise this idea won't bring you any physical harm? The only thing you'll be in danger of is getting too attached to your sexy next-door neighbor."

"What does Oliver have to do with this?" I hold back a grin as I refer to one of my other next-door neighbors.

Kai narrows his eyes at me then gently tugs on a strand of my long, brown hair. "Let's get something straight. The only sexy next-door neighbor you have is me. Got it?"

The thought of Kyler Meyers, Kai's older brother, who I've had a crush on forever, pops into my head. I was supposed to be on a date with him tonight—our very first date to be exact—but I had to cancel because I couldn't quit sobbing. I didn't tell Kyler that, though. I just told him something came up. He was really sweet about it and asked me out next weekend. Of course, I said yes. I just hope I feel better by then.

Not wanting to get into that with Kai since Kyler is a touchy subject for him, I heave a dramatic sigh. "Fine, my one and only sexy next-door neighbor, what's your awesome idea?"

His eyes light up. "I was thinking, if you went to live with your grandma, I could give you a ride to and from school."

My heart melts like warm chocolate. That would be the sweetest thing a guy has ever done for me—well, except for when he stopped the whole straightjacket rumor Hannah tried to spread about me. That one is pretty high up there. "You'd do that for me?"

"Of course. That's what *friends* do for each other, right?"

The way he says *friends*, as if the word is amusing, turns me into an overanalyzing, read-between-the-lines-way-too-much girl. Why did it sound like he finds it funny that we're friends? Or maybe I'm just over-thinking it. Why do I care?

Hormones, dude, hormones. Get a grip on yourself.

"While I appreciate the offer, I'm not sure I feel comfortable with you doing that," I tell him, despite not wanting to turn down his offer. "I mean, you'd have to get up, like, an hour earlier than you normally do."

"An hour isn't that big of a deal," he insists, picking up the remote and shutting off the television.

"You're not a morning person, Kai. You told me the other day that you hate waking up any earlier than noon, that you turn into a cranky monster."

"I didn't say cranky monster. I said asshole. And that's

only on weekends. I get up at, like, seven thirty on weekdays."

"Only when you go to school on time. You're usually late."

"Well, I guess I'll have to start being on time." He gives a casual shrug, pretending it's not a big deal, even though it is.

At least, it is for me.

"You really don't have to do this," I say. The last thing I want to do is force him to drive all the way across Sunnyvale to pick my sorry butt up and get himself on a schedule when he's clearly an I'll-do-what-I-want-whenever-I-want-to kind of guy. "It might be good for me to start a new school, anyway. It'll force me to make friends without your ever-so-awesome unicorn guidance." I press my palms together and bow to him.

He chuckles, shaking his head. "It's really not a big deal." He gives my knee a squeeze. "So just accept my offer."

My knee jolts from his touch, and I hastily clear my throat, unsure how to respond.

While he keeps referring to us as friends, I'm not so sure our relationship is that simple. Yeah, Kai and I are friends, but we've drunkenly kissed once and almost kissed another time. Despite the kiss being brief, I swear to God fireworks and explosions burst through me. I felt like

I'd stepped into one of those sappy rom-coms or something. According to Kai, though, he kisses everyone when he's drunk. But then he almost kissed me in our old hideout, a hollowed out tree trunk, and that was while he was completely sober. He hasn't tried to make up an excuse for that one. We're just pretending it never happened.

"So, what do you say? Will you please let me be your chauffeur?" he asks, drawing me back to reality.

His fingers are still on my knee, tracing delicate circles across my skin, his fingertips moving higher on my thigh toward the bottom of my skirt. I'm not even sure he knows he's doing it. I should probably wiggle my leg before he unknowingly feels me up, but I can't seem to move or breathe. I can't do anything, really, except idiotically gape at his fingers.

Noting where I'm staring, his gaze drops to his hand. He stares for a second or two before swiftly withdrawing and coughing into his hand.

"Sorry, I…"

Silence stretches between us.

Um… Can you say awkward?

It's kind of weird since Kai usually just owns whatever he does.

My skin is on fire as I clear my throat. "No worries."

"Besides, starting a new school your senior year would suck balls," he continues as if nothing happened. "Everyone will already have their own thing going on.

It'd be better if you just finished here and then started over in college."

"Are you sure you want to make that kind of commitment, though?"

"I never commit to anything aloud until I'm one hundred percent sure I'm down with it."

"Okay. I accept your offer to be my chauffeur." An ounce of weight lifts from my shoulders. Now if I could just get rid of the rest, life would be all cookies and vanilla sprinkle frosting. "But you know what that means, right? I get to boss you around."

His eyes narrow to slits, but it's a playful move. "I take back the chauffeur thing. How about just a *friend* helping another *friend*."

Oh, for the love of all zombies, why does he keep saying *friend* like that? Every time he does, it makes me think of our kiss and almost kiss, something friends don't do.

"Why are you blushing, Isa?" Humor dances in his eyes.

"I'm not." I duck my head, reaching for the stack of DVDs on the floor and hiding my blush. "Can we watch one more movie before I deal with this moving out thing? I need to think about what I'm going to say to everyone."

His gaze practically burns a hole in the side of my head. "If that's what you want."

I nod, scoop up the DVDs, and straighten. "I'm avoiding going back to my house. I'm kind of scared."

"I don't blame you." He does that whole intense, smoldering, I'm-trying-to-burn-a-hole-into-your-head-so-I-can-read-your-thoughts look on me just long enough to make me squirmy. It's a breath of fresh air when he finally looks away, snatching the DVDs from my hand. "Which one are we watching?"

"I'll let you pick since you let me pick the last one."

He sorts through the DVDs and ends up selecting *28 Days Later*.

"You really want to watch another zombie movie?" I ask as he gets up to put the DVD into the player.

He feeds the disc in. "Sure. Zombies are cool."

My chest constricts again, but in a different, more welcoming way. "Kai..."

"Yeah?" He fiddles with the buttons on the DVD player.

My heart pitter-patters. "Thanks for taking care of me today."

"It's no big deal." He shrugs, but I swear to God I hear a smile in his voice. He presses play then returns to the sofa. "I mean, yeah, it's kind of a pain in the ass to take care of your sugar and zombie addiction." He sits down beside me and playfully bumps his shoulder against mine. "For a minute there, things got intense. I was worried you were going to turn into a gremlin and bite my hand off if

I didn't let you dump the Milk Duds into the popcorn, but I think I deflated the situation pretty well."

"They taste better together," I protest. "The heat makes them all melty, gooey, good."

"Melty, huh?" He drapes his arm across the back of the sofa and rests his hand behind me. "That sounds like a word that belongs in the Awesome Isabella Dictionary."

Smiling, I reach for the popcorn bowl on the end table beside me. I place it on my lap and stuff a handful into my mouth as the movie starts.

But around five minutes in, my mind is elsewhere, which is a first for me while watching a zombie movie. But I let my temporary insanity slide since I have a lot on my mind.

I want to believe my mom isn't dead, that what Lynn told me was her sick, twisted way of messing with me. But even if my real mom isn't dead, I worry about why everyone thinks she's this horrible person. What could she have possibly done to make them think that? What happened fourteen years ago when I left the life I was raised in and came to live with my dad, the evil witch of the Anders home, and her wicked wench sidekick daughter?

Abruptly, Kai stiffens beside me. I think he's freaking out over the gory scene on the screen until I note he's staring at the corner of the room. The only thing there is a miniature gnome, so unless Kai's suddenly developed a fear of beady-eyed little creatures, I'm guessing he's stressing over something else.

"Everything okay?" I ask him.

He blinks at me. "Huh?"

"You were dazing off." I try to read his vibe, but Kai can be so mysterious sometimes. "We can change this if you're bored." I start to get up, but he clasps a hand on my leg, forcing me to stay put.

"Relax. I said I was cool with watching the movie, and I meant it." He only releases me from his grip when I chillax. "Now watch the movie."

I do what he says, but ten minutes later, he's zoning off into empty space again, looking extremely bothered. Kai's in some kind of trouble with a guy who goes by the name T, and I wonder if he's concerned over that. He won't talk about it, though. Trust me, I've tried.

I can't help thinking of a few hours ago when he hugged me in front of his house and winced like I was hurting him. When I asked him about it, he cracked a joke about my tiny arms giving him booboos. Could T have hurt him?

"Isa, would you please stop staring at me?" His gaze glides to me, and he bites on his bottom lip. "You're giving me a complex."

"I know that's not true. No one could ever give Ego Man a complex," I retort, using the superhero nickname I gave him earlier today, trying to lighten his mood.

"That's not true." He steadily holds my gaze. "Every superhero has a kryptonite."

"You're saying me staring at you is your kryptonite?" I ask with an arched brow.

He shrugs but doesn't say anything, zoning off again.

"Are you sure you're okay?" I ask.

He nods then gets up and heads for the doorway like it's on fire. "I'm going to go and make some more popcorn. I'll be right back."

I look down at the bowl in my lap, half full of popcorn. He obviously wanted to leave the room, but why? What is he hiding from me?

2

KAI

I wake up on the sofa with a warm body pressed against mine. At first, I'm confused as hell. Then I catch the faintest scent of popcorn, and the fogginess in my mind gradually lifts. Zombie movies. Popcorn. Milk Duds. *Isa.*

She's fast asleep with her head resting on my arm, her hand on my chest, and our legs are so tangled I can't tell where hers start and mine end.

We must've fallen asleep during the movie. I don't know if that's a good thing or not. I mean, sure, it's a fantasy come true to wake up with her practically lying on top of me. But I'm supposed to be keeping this thing with us strictly in the friend zone until I can get my act together, and she can get over this stupid idea that she's supposed to be with Kyler. Plus, her elbow is putting pressure on the ribs T cracked his knuckles against yesterday. I'm pretty sure one might be broken, but there's nothing I can do about it. I've broken a couple of ribs before in football and know the healing process consists of taking it easy and not moving the area much.

I'm deliberating what I should do when Isa lets out a soft moan and nuzzles closer to me.

Fuck it. This is definitely a good thing.

I rub my eyes with my free hand and relax, wondering what time it is. Sunlight is peering through the cracks in the curtains, so it has to be at least seven o'clock. I should probably wake her up and explain that we fell asleep. But it's too nice holding her, and I end up just lying there, watching her sleep like a creeper.

She looks so relaxed with her face resting in the crook of my arm, her lips parted as she softly breathes. I wish I could let her lie like this all day, but eventually, she's going to wake up, and I'm going to have to tell her that her mom's alive but in a prison in Virginia for murder charges.

I tuck a strand of her hair behind her ear then graze my knuckles across her cheek. Her skin is so soft and warm—

"What the hell's going on?" Kyler's annoying voice cuts through the moment.

I let out a frustrated grunt. *Great. Here comes drama.*

I fire a shut-the-hell-up look at him. "Keep your voice down, or you'll wake her up."

Kyler's face turns bright red. "Why is she here with you when she was supposed to be on a date with me last night?"

I hesitate. I'm not sure how much Kyler knows about what's going on with Isa. The longer I remain silent, the redder Kyler's face gets. I consider not uttering a word, letting him come up with all kinds of ideas about what Isa and I were doing last night. It's not like the two of them are officially together. They haven't even been out on a date yet. But I'm not sure Isa waking up to Kyler all pissed off at her is a great idea.

"Would you chill out?" I say, resisting an eye roll. "We were watching a movie last night and fell asleep. Nothing happened."

He crosses his arms, dumbfounded. "She blew me off so she could stay here and watch a movie with *you*?"

"No, you dumbass." I carefully slip my arm out from underneath Isa and stand up, wincing as my ribs groan in protest. "Something happened yesterday that upset her, so we hung out, and I distracted her with a zombie movie marathon." When he continues to look irritated, I add, "Nothing happened." I want to add, *but it wouldn't matter if something did happen, because she's not yours.*

His jaw ticks. "Why didn't she talk to me?"

I keep my elbow to my side, hoping to reduce some of the pain in my ribs. "Huh?"

"When whatever happened that upset her, why did she ask you for help instead of me?"

"She didn't come to me. I was just there when the shit hit the fan." It nearly kills me to say it, to tell him that Isa didn't choose me over him. I was just the one she ran into first.

For as long as I can remember, Kyler has gotten whatever he wanted whenever he wanted: from his choice in girlfriends to positions on the team to making everyone in our school worship him. He's always been better than me in sports and hooked up with girls I liked. I put an end to the sports problem by quitting, and it was a huge relief. I was tired of living in his shadow and wanted to find my own thing that didn't include being compared to my older brother. As for dating the girls I liked, sure, it pissed me off, but I got over it.

Isa, though... She's different. She's seriously the sweetest, coolest, most beautiful girl I've ever known. I just wish I could've seen that back in seventh grade, but I was a stupid kid who wanted to fit in with the in-crowd. Still, I liked her way before Kyler did, before she started wearing makeup and dressing more like a girl. I know the only reason he likes her is because he thinks she's hot. He doesn't even know anything about her.

Kyler gradually unstiffens. "So maybe she would've

talked to me if she hadn't run into you first." An arrogant smile rises across his face.

I want to punch him in the face, but I don't want Isa to wake up to a fight breaking out. Plus, more than likely, my dad would come in and chew my ass off. He can't stand me right now and is looking for any reason to punish me. I think he wants to kick me out of the house.

"You're eighteen years old," he said to me a couple of months ago after I came home trashed. "Maybe it's time for you to move out."

I wanted to argue that I wasn't ready to move out, but my pride got in the way. "Maybe I should."

He gave me the same condescending look he always gives whenever he's about to prove how much of a loser I am. "Well, you better start looking for places, then." He slapped the newspaper onto the kitchen table in front of me. "Good luck trying to find a place when your dumbass doesn't have any money."

"Honey, watch your language," my mom intervened as she piled fruit into the blender. "Kai, what I think your father is saying is that, if you can't clean up your act, we may have to take a more drastic route. We love you, but I'm not going to stand around and watch you throw your life away."

"This is so fucking stupid." I shoved the newspaper away as I rose to my feet. "Kyler got drunk all the time when he was my age, and you guys never did anything."

"Kyler was also the captain of the football and basketball teams and was an honor roll student." My father looked at me with disgust. "You barely even go to school anymore. You're wasting your life, partying and coming home wasted every weekend. If you keep going down this path, you're going to end up a deadbeat, pumping gas for a living."

"No one pumps gas for people anymore," I mumbled then left the kitchen before he could ream into me more.

"Umm…" Isa's startled voice yanks me away from the memory.

I glance over my shoulder at her.

She's sitting up, fussing with her hair, and her eyes are darting back and forth between me and Kyler. "What happened?" Her bleary gaze lands on me. "Did we fall asleep watching the movie?"

I nod. "Apparently, even you can get tired of zombies."

She rolls her eyes like that's the silliest thing she's ever heard. "I'm not tired of zombies. Just tired." The second her eyes go back to Kyler, she goes from playful to shy. "Hey."

"Hey… So, you canceled our date last night so you could sleep with my brother?" He winks at her. "I think that might be a first for me."

Isa's cheeks turn pink. "I didn't sleep with him. Well, I did, but not on purpose. We just sort of fell asleep while we were watching a movie."

Kyler chuckles then pushes past me and sits down beside her on the sofa. "Relax, I'm just messing with you. Kai told me what happened."

"Oh, good." She looks away from him as she runs her fingers below her eyes, trying to wipe away some smeared makeup. "Sorry I had to cancel our date, but a bunch of stuff happened, and I would've been a downer to be around."

"It's okay." He brushes a strand of her hair out of her face. "Is it anything you want to talk about?"

I stand there, hoping Isa will duck away from his touch, but I can tell she likes it by the way her eyelashes flutter.

I don't want to wait around to hear her answer. I don't think I could take it if she told him about her mom and what's going on with her family.

"I have to go." I back toward the doorway, tucking my hands into my pockets. "You two kids have fun. And don't do anything I wouldn't do."

Isa gives me a pleading look like she doesn't want me to leave yet. I almost stay, but when Kyler puts his hand on her knee, I know, if I stick around, I'll lose my shit.

After I leave the den, I go into the kitchen to grab something to eat. As I'm pulling out a couple of Toaster Strudels from the freezer, I check the time on the clock. Shit. I'm supposed to be at Big Doug's place already. Last night, I told him about the mess I've gotten into with T.

He told me to come over today because he might have some work for me that would allow me to make some cash fast and get T paid back ASAP.

I've done some work for Big Doug before, but I stopped when we almost got busted while tapping into a bank's security cameras. To this day, I'm still not sure why we were doing it, but if we'd gotten caught, I could've ended up in jail. That's why I hate that I have to go back into that world. But, at the moment, I don't see another alternative.

I shove the Toaster Strudels in the toaster, pop some painkillers, and then head toward the stairs.

As I'm rounding the corner in the hallway, Isa walks out of the den. The two of us collide hard.

"Aw, fuck," I curse, hunching over from the pain radiating through my side.

"Oh, my God. I'm sorry. I didn't see…" She trails off.

I glance up at her, wondering what she's doing.

Her furious gaze is fastened on me, and her hands are on her hips.

"What the hell is that look for?" I try to keep my voice light, but I sound strained. I force myself to stand up straight and keep my arm at my side. "All right, what'd I do now?"

Her pointed gaze travels to my injured side. "I knew you were hurt. Why didn't you tell me?"

"Yeah, I'm hurt because we just crashed into each other," I lie, sidestepping to squeeze by her.

She sidesteps and blocks my path with her arms stretched out to the sides of her. "No way. You're not going anywhere until you tell me what's wrong."

I bite back my amusement over how unintentionally cute she's being right now. "And what if I don't? What're you going to do?"

She mulls it over for a second or two. Then her arm darts forward. She grips the bottom of my shirt and lifts it up to peer underneath.

I should probably stop her before she sees the gnarly bruise on my side, but as her knuckles graze the bottom of my stomach, I get too turned on to care.

"Oh, my God, Kai," she gasps at the sight of the purplish-yellow marks dotting my ribcage, reaching forward and tentatively touching the area.

My muscles constrict from the contact, and she immediately jerks back, but I catch her hand and hold it against my side.

Her gaze elevates to my face, uncertainty filling her eyes. "Who hurt you?"

"It's not a big deal. I just got into a tiny, little fight." I wink at her. "But you should see the other guy."

"Was this..." She struggles for words, her fingers trembling against my side. "Did that T guy do this to you?"

I open my mouth to lie, but then I realize I don't want to lie to her any more than I already have. "Yeah, and—"

"Hey, so I was thinking, since you didn't want to go home yet, we could go get some breakfast," Kyler says, strolling out of the den.

Isa steps back from me. "Are you sure? I don't want to put you out," she says to Kyler.

I grind my teeth. If Kyler knows she doesn't want to go home, then does that mean she told him what's going on? Jealousy burns inside me, and I hate the feeling so much. I've spent way too many years carrying it around. It's part of why I decided to quit sports, change my life, who I was.

After muttering a goodbye, I haul ass to the stairway. I half-expect Isa to call out to me, but she doesn't. It's probably for the better. I need to focus on getting out of this mess with T right now before I even attempt to go down any sort of romantic relationship road with Isa. At least, that's what I try to convince myself, but deep down, all I want to do is go back, grab Isa, and kiss her. And for real this time, when we're both sober and can enjoy it.

As I enter my room, my phone buzzes from inside the pocket of my black jeans. I dig it out as I rummage through my dresser for a clean shirt.

T: If you don't get me my grand in three weeks, yesterday is going to seem like a fucking cakewalk.

I swallow hard. A thousand! Mother fucker! I didn't

realize Bradon owed T that much. How the hell am I supposed to come up with a thousand bucks in three weeks? There's no way I can make that much in three weeks working for Big Doug.

I have no clue what I'm going to do, but I better come up with a plan. And fast.

3

ISABELLA

Kai walks away from Kyler and me like we're carrying some viral disease and are about to infect him. I open my mouth to call after him because I'm not about to let him leave until he explains what kind of trouble he's gotten into, but Kyler snags my hand and steers me in the direction of the kitchen before I get a chance.

Normally, I'd be all over the fact that Kyler Meyers is holding my hand, but my mind is on Kai and those bruises. They looked really bad, and he seemed to be in a lot of pain. I wonder if his ribs are broken.

"Just let him go," Kyler says. "When he gets like this, it's better if you just leave him alone."

"Gets like what?" I wonder if Kyler knows what's going on with Kai.

Kyler shrugs as he leads me to the mudroom then

releases my hand. "Pissy and upset. He's been like this since we were kids. He gets into trouble and then sulks about it and makes everyone miserable."

I start to slip on my shoes. "Do you know why he's upset?"

He sits down on a wooden bench to slip on his sneakers. "Who knows? He's been a real asshole lately. My parents think he's on drugs. I heard them talking about sending him to rehab or something."

I shift my weight, feeling uncomfortable talking to Kyler about Kai, like I'm betraying Kai. "Kai's not on drugs, Kyler."

He peers up from tying his shoelaces, brushing strands of his light brown hair away from his forehead. "How do you know that?"

"He told me he doesn't do them." Anymore. But Kyler doesn't need to know about that part.

"And you just believed him?"

"He's my friend. He wouldn't lie to me."

Kyler stares at me dubiously, seeming unhappy with my answer. Then he pushes the irritation aside and rises to his feet. "Maybe you're right. Maybe he's not on drugs, but there's definitely something going on with him."

I keep my lips fused. It feels wrong to be talking to Kyler about Kai. Now, if I find out what's going on with Kai and it's really bad, then that's a different story. I'll do what I have to do to help him, even if it means getting help from his family.

"Where do you want to get breakfast?" he asks, grabbing a jacket from a coatrack.

"Anywhere works for me." I glance down at my wrinkled clothes. My breath tastes like rotten broccoli, and I'm sure my makeup is smeared all over my face. "Can I go home and change first?"

"Of course." He opens the door and motions for me to go out first. "But I thought you didn't want to go home."

Very true. I don't want to go home, and honestly, I doubt I'm allowed to. Still, I should get my stuff. If only there were a way to get into my room without actually having to go through the house...

I dare a look over at the driveway of my house. Hannah's car is parked behind Lynn's and my dad's. They're all home, probably sitting around the kitchen table, eating breakfast and plotting how they're going to continue trying to destroy me.

While I'm still unsure who the unknown texter is, I have a feeling it may be one of the three of them. I have no clue why they're doing this to me, but I'm worried about what kind of torment waits for me in the future.

Kyler joins me outside, closing the door behind him. "Isa, can I... Do you mind if I ask why you don't want to go home?"

I haven't told him anything, and I really don't want to.

While I have a major, borderline-stalker crush on Kyler, I don't know him well enough to trust him that much. I want to. Like, a ton. But establishing trust requires getting to know him as something other than the gorgeous, popular guy who lives next door, talked to me a few times, and gave me a rose once.

"I'm just fighting with my parents." I decide to go with the partial truth. I eyeball the banister of the deck attached to my bedroom. If only I had a Pegasus or fairy wings so I could fly right up there or perhaps Spiderman web fingers so I could scale the wall... Wait a minute... "Do you, by chance, have a ladder?"

He tracks my gaze, and his expression plummets. "You seriously want to climb up there just to avoid your parents?"

I bob my head up and down. "It's better that way. Trust me." Yeah, it might be a little drastic, but it's way better than dealing with the drama waiting for me inside that house.

"If that's what you want, then you got it." He rubs his hands together, backing down the stairs and toward the garage. "One ladder coming up."

I smile at him gratefully then plant my butt on the railing and wait for him to return. A light fall breeze kisses the air, and clouds shadow the sky. It's the beginning of October, and some of the neighbors have already pulled out the decorations, the Meyer's yard included.

Inflatable pumpkins and plastic tombstones cover the front yard, and a giant spider is perched on the basketball hoop. I remember all those times I sat out on my balcony, watching Kyler play basketball in his driveway and wishing I were with him. And now I am over here. Funny how life changes. The thought gives me the tiniest drop of peace in the sea of depression swishing around inside me.

Optimism, I remind myself. Lynn may have said all those horrible things about my mom, but like Kai said, she's not the most reliable source. As a result, until I have the actual facts in front of me, I can't believe my mom's dead or that she was a bad person.

I just start to relax until the side door to my house swings open, and Hannah walks out. At first, she's too busy texting to notice me sitting on the Meyer's porch. But when she drops her phone into her purse and reaches to open her car door, her eyes drift next-door and zero in right on me. A series of emotions flash across her face—confusion, shock, anger—and then her lips curl.

She strolls up to the fence, sneering. "You know stalking's illegal, right?"

I fold my arms around myself, starting to shrink away. But then I force myself to lift up my chin. *No. No more cowering.* "I could say the same thing to you."

She rolls her eyes. "Is this about that stupid text thing?

Because I already told you that wasn't me. I have way better things thing to do with my life, and you would know that if you had a life." A malicious look glimmers in her eyes. "And FYI, you might want to look in a mirror. You look like shit. Then again, you always look like shit."

Anger boils inside me like lava. Usually, I bite my tongue and try to rise above or whatever, but after everything that went down yesterday, my willpower snaps. I'm furious at her, at Lynn ... at my dad for lying to me, for never sticking up for me, for letting me live with people who belittled my self-worth every day for years.

"What's your problem?" I hop off the railing and step off the deck, striding toward the fence. "I've never done anything to you, yet you've always hated me."

She barks a disdainful laugh. "Your mother almost ruined my parents' marriage. I have every right to hate you."

My muscles ravel into knots. How long has she known about my mom? How much does she know? "They're not just your parents. Your dad's still my dad, Hannah."

"If he had his way, he wouldn't be." She flips her blonde hair off her shoulder. "All you do is remind him of the biggest mistake of his life. No wonder he can't even stand to look at you." Her brows rise as she assesses me, her face pinching in repulsion. "But most people can't.

You're worthless. I know it. My mom knows it. *My* dad knows it."

All the rage I've bottled up for nearly eighteen years explodes. Before I even realize what I'm doing, I lift my leg to climb over the fence.

Hannah's eyes widen in surprise, and she trips back, causing one of her heels to get stuck in the grass. I'm not even one hundred percent sure what I'm going to do to her: slap her, push her down, mess up her hair, force her to watch me break her manicured nails off. But before I can get over the fence, arms wrap around my waist and gently pull me back.

"As much as I think you deserve to do whatever you're about to do," Kai whispers in my ear. "She's not worth the trouble you'll get in for kicking her ass."

Hannah scoffs. "Like she could kick my ass."

Keeping one arm looped around my waist, Kai moves beside me and smirks at Hannah. "Then why do you look like you're about to piss your pants?"

Hannah glares at Kai. "You're such an asshole, Kai. Why are you even here? No one asked you to come over here and be a jerk."

"Why are you here?" He quips. "No one asked you to come over and bitch at Isa in that shrill voice of yours." When her eyes shoot daggers at Kai, he grins in satisfaction. "So, here's a thought: why don't you walk away before I tell Isa about what you did two summers ago and give her all the ammo she needs to make your life a living hell. And while you're at it, stop sending her those texts."

I have no idea what he's referring to, but I'm so thankful he's standing up for me that I want to turn around and hug him.

"How many times do I have to say this! I didn't send Isa any texts!" Hannah's expression darkens, her voice lowering an octave. "And how dare you threaten me?"

"I didn't threaten so much as warn you that I'll tell everyone your dirty little secret." He flashes his pearly whites at her. "But if you want to look at it like that, then go right ahead."

Steam practically shoots out of Hannah's ears. "No one ever threatens me. You're so going to pay for this." She spins around to leave but then spots Kyler coming out of the garage with a ladder. She goes from the Ice Queen to cotton candy sweet, plastering on a smile. "Hey, Kyler. I didn't know you were home this weekend. I thought you said you were going on a trip with your friends or something."

Kai's hand falls from my waist, and he puts some distance between us.

Kyler sets the ladder down beside the fence and dusts off his hands, his gaze skimming the three of us. "I... um... I was supposed to, but my friends... bailed out at the last second."

I think he might be lying to her, and even though it

might make me a little twisted, I find an odd sense of happiness in that fact.

"Oh." For a brief second, rage blazes in her eyes, but the look fades, and an exaggerated smile returns. "Good, then I guess you can take me out today after all."

Kyler massages the back of his neck tensely. "Actually, I already made plans with someone else."

Her smile goes *poof*. "With who?" she snaps. "It better not be that slut, Carissa."

"It's not her…" Kyler shifts his weight uneasily.

I'm not sure whether to take his hesitancy personally. Is he ashamed he's going out with me? Or is he sparing me the hell that's going to follow when Hannah finds out?

Kyler gives me a sidelong glance, and his eyes carry a silent question: *what should I tell her?* I'm not sure. While I don't want to keep our date … hanging out … going to breakfast … whatever we're doing today, a secret. I also don't want to give Hannah more of a reason to torment me.

I never get to decide my answer, though, because Hannah notices Kyler looking in my direction, and Pandora's box flies open.

"Are you effing kidding me!" she shouts, her voice so loud the neighbor across the street looks up from watering his lawn. "Her! That… that loser!"

"What the heck is your problem?" Kyler says at the

same time Kai warns, "Guess just threatening you wasn't enough." Me, I think about jumping over that fence again, going all ninja on her, and kicking her ass. Kai must sense this, too, because his fingers fold around my arm and he holds onto me.

Hannah shakes her head, fuming mad. "Don't pretend like you two haven't thought the same thing. Up until she came back this summer, you both used to make fun of her all the time."

It grows so quiet I can hear Mr. Normbert's sprinklers turning on just down the street. I feel so small, like these tiny fairy statues my grandma Stephy used to collect back when my grandpa was still alive. She kept them in front of her house near the tulip bed. I thought they were so cute and used to sit out there and pretend they were my magical friends who granted wishes. One day, Hannah caught me, called me a freak, and stomped all over them until they were nothing more than broken glass.

"Actually, I never did." Kai inches toward the fence, getting close to Hannah. "You've always known what I thought of Isa, at least since *two summers ago.*"

Hannah gives Kai the dirtiest look. Then, shooting one last glare in my direction, she turns her back on us, muttering something under her breath as she storms toward her car. She yanks the door open, revs the engine, and then peels out of the driveway, leaving tire marks on the concrete.

I'm starting to let out a relieved breath when the door to my house opens.

My dad steps out and looks right at me. "Isabella Anders, get your ass over here right now. You and I need to talk. And that's not a request. Either get over here now, or I'll call the cops."

4

ISABELLA

I WANT TO TELL HIM TO LEAVE ME ALONE, THAT WE HAVE nothing to talk about, but the threat of calling the cops scares the words right out of me.

"Fine. I'm headed over," I holler to my dad then turn to Kyler, feeling awkward. Unlike Kai, Kyler didn't deny that he called me a loser behind my back with Hannah and her friends. I'm not sure what to do with that. "I think I have to take a rain check on breakfast."

"I can wait for you," Kyler offers. "I don't have anything to do today, anyway."

"Are you sure?" I ask. "It might take a while."

He nods, stuffing his hands into the pockets of his dark denim jeans. "I need to talk to you about some stuff, anyway."

"Okay…." *Talk to me about what exactly?* "I'll come over

here when I'm done talking to my dad." I wave at him then hike toward the end of the driveway.

Kai matches my steps, strolling along beside me. "Maybe you shouldn't go over there."

"I think I have to"—I halt at the edge of the fence—"if for nothing else than to get my stuff before they decide to throw it away."

The wind blows strands of his hair up, and he runs his hand over his head to flatten them back down as he stares off across the street. "I don't like this."

"Kai, I'll be fine. I'm sure he just wants to tell me I have to move out."

Tension is set in his jawline as his gaze shifts to me. "I'm worried about you… that… that they're going to try to break you apart. I mean, why would he threaten to call the cops on you?"

"I'm sure that was just to get me to come over without a fight," I tell him, even though I don't quite believe the words myself. "It's not like I've done anything wrong. I'll be fine." I flex my muscles. "I've got skin made of steel, baby," I attempt to joke but miss the mark, my voice falling flat like a deflated balloon. "I'll call you after I'm done talking to him, okay? I think we need to talk about some stuff, anyway." *Like why this T guy beat you up.*

"Fine," he grumbles then shakes his head multiple times, mumbling something about having a bad feeling.

I start to leave but then pause as an overwhelming

need surfaces. "Kai, thanks for everything you did back there with Hannah, for standing up for me. No one's ever done that... It means a lot."

"I was just doing what friends should do for each other." He doesn't use a funny tone when he says *friends* this time. He sounds dead serious and so is the intensity in his eyes.

I walk away with a hundred butterflies going wild inside my stomach and a tornado of confusion whipping through my mind. I feel like I'm tumbling into the unknown, down, down, down the rabbit hole into madness where nothing makes sense anymore. I have no idea who I am, who I want to be, what I want.

The feeling only amplifies when I enter my house, and my dad isn't in the kitchen. Instead, Lynn is sitting at the table with a stack of papers in front of her and an arrogant grin on her face.

"Isa, have a seat," she says, gesturing at the chair next to her.

I remain near the back door. "Where's my dad? He said he needed to talk to me, not you."

"Your dad's upstairs, and he won't be a part of this conversation, because he doesn't want to have to deal with you. I've been kind enough to volunteer for the position, though." Her calm voice sends a chill down my spine. "So. Sit. Down."

I momentarily dither before taking a seat in the chair

farthest away from her. I tuck my hands underneath the table so she can't see me fidgeting and wait for her to say something.

She drags the silence out for as long as possible, as if she knows it's driving me crazy. "Yesterday, after you put your hands on me, your father and I sat down to discuss how violent you've gotten."

"How violent I've gotten?" I shake my head. "I pushed you once, Lynn, and that's mild to the abuse you and Hannah have done to me over the years."

Her hard gaze narrows on me. "No one in this house has ever laid a hand on you."

"I'm talking about verbal abuse, Lynn. Words can sometimes be just as harmful as actions," I repeat what Kai said to me last night.

Her fingers curl inward. For a horrifying moment, I think she's going to hit me. But she presses her knuckles against the edge of the stack of papers and shoves the paper across the table to me.

"After your father and I discussed your violent behavior," she continues on with her speech, "we decided the best thing for everyone is if you go to a boarding school that specializes in troubled teens."

My heart slams against my chest as I read the top of one of the papers. "You're sending me to *Montana!*" I shove back from the table. "No way. I'm not going."

She sits there with her perfect posture and a sickeningly pleased look on her face. "You're still a minor, and as your guardian, you have no choice but to do what I say."

"You're not my only guardian," I say then bolt from the kitchen. "Dad!" My feet stomp against the steps as I run upstairs. "Dad, you can't let her send me away." I hurry to his bedroom door and pound my fist against it. "Dad, please. Don't let her do this."

"I'm not letting her do anything," he responds through the closed door. "I agree with Lynn. You need to go, Isa. It's for the best."

"The best for who?" I grab the doorknob and jerk on the door, but it's locked.

I pound on the door a few times before giving up and running to my room. I try to call my grandma Stephy, but she doesn't answer. I leave her a message then text Indigo, even though there's only, like, a one percent chance she'll read the text while she's at work. When she doesn't respond, I grab a few duffel bags from my closet and start throwing what I can inside: clothes, shoes, my sketchbook, art supplies, my computer. After I've stuffed the bags full, I dig my stash of cash out from the top dresser drawer and stuff it into my back pocket. Then I sling the bags over my shoulders and rush out of my room.

When I make it to the bottom of the stairway, Lynn is waiting for me, blocking my path to the back door.

"You're not going anywhere." She crosses her arms, her overly plucked brows arching. "You're staying here until tomorrow morning, and then your father and I are driving you up to Montana. And if you so much as show any signs of getting violent, we won't hesitate to call the police."

I have an unsettling feeling she's hoping I'll try to push her again, give her a reason to call the police.

"I'm not staying here," I say in the calmest voice I can muster. "And I'm not going to the school in Montana. I'll be eighteen in a couple of months. I can live with Grandma Stephy until then."

"Until you're eighteen, your father and I tell you what to do, not the other way around. You won't be living with your grandma Stephy. You'll be living in Montana, far, far away where you can't hurt anyone." Her lips curl into a smile. "And where you can't turn into your dirty whore of a mother."

I almost throw down right there, but at the last second, I manage to see through the blindingly hot anger. She wants me to get mad. She wants me to hurt her. She wants me to be exactly who she's telling me I am.

"Is that why you've treated me so crappy?" I snap, shocking her and myself. "Because my dad cheated on you with my mom?"

Her lips curl into a malicious grin as her hand darts forward. She snags hold of my arm, and her fingers dig into my flesh. "You ungrateful little brat. If you only knew what your mother did… how much she really ruined this family, how sick and twisted she really is… I could tell you, too. Watch you break. But I'm not going to just yet. It's so much more fun watching you suffer, watching your own father destroy your life. And he does it so easily because he secretly despises you and everything you represent."

My lungs tighten, sucking the oxygen out of my lungs. I can barely breathe. I see spots. If I don't get air into my lungs, I'll pass out.

Don't pass out. Don't pass out. If you pass out, God knows where you'll wake up. Just get out of here. Now.

Sucking in a deep breath, I wrench my arm away from her. Then I grip the banister and hoist myself over it like a freaking badass mofo hurdler. I'm on the bottom step, so it's not a far fall or anything, but my ninja move throws her off. She gapes at me in shock as I run toward the front door. It takes a second or two before I hear the sound of her footsteps chasing after me. I don't slow down, bursting out the front door. Then I sprint down the sidewalk straight for the Meyers house, crossing my fingers that Kai will be there to give me a ride to my grandma Stephy's house where I know I'll be safe for now.

Dropping my bags on the back deck of the Meyers', I knock on the door while throwing a quick glance back at my house. Thank my lucky charms, Lynn hasn't come out yet. Hopefully, she'll give up and just let me leave. Although, I highly doubt it. Whatever happened between my real mom, my dad, and her has caused her to set out on a mission to destroy me. I just wish I knew if Lynn's hatred stems solely from the affair of if there's more to it than that.

Every bone in my body excruciatingly aches as I replay her words over and over again. I've always known I wasn't my dad's favorite, but to hear her say it aloud... so venomously... It stings like poison in my veins.

I look down at my wrist where she grabbed me. Red marks dot my skin. How can she say that my violence is a problem after she did this? Knowing Lynn, though, she'll probably lie and tell my dad it was self-defense. When I really think about it, over the course of my life, she's done that a lot—twisted stories to make me look like the bad one. And my dad believes them so easily.

By the time the Meyers' door opens, I'm tumbling into a hole of self-pity and loathing. But I claw my way out of it when I see Kyler in the doorway, taking in the sight of me out of breath, my eyes wild, and worry creases his forehead.

"Are you okay?" he asks.

I fight back my tears. "Um... Is Kai here?" I feel bad when he looks hurt, but I'd rather talk to Kai right now since he knows what's going on.

"He left just." He assesses me with concern. "What did you need him to do? Whatever it is, I can help you. Just trust me, okay?"

I stuff my hands into the pockets of my jacket. "Um, can you drive me to my grandma's? I really need to talk to her." It's the best I can give him for now.

He doesn't miss a beat. "Sure. Give me two seconds."

He rushes back into the house, leaving the door open. He returns two seconds later, wearing a blue hoodie and carrying a set of keys. Without saying anything, he picks up my bags and jogs down the back steps toward the garage. I follow him, repeatedly glancing over at my house. It's quiet. Too quiet. I worry Lynn might be up to something, like calling me in as a runaway. I consider going home, but just the thought of doing so makes my stomach churn.

After Kyler and I get into his car, he backs onto the road and pulls out onto the main road.

"Do you remember where she lives?" I ask, clipping in my seatbelt.

He nods, cranking up the heat. "At Sunnyvale Bay Community, right?"

Nodding, I recline back in the seat. "Yeah. And thanks for doing this."

He opens his mouth to say something, but my phone rings, cutting him off. I fumble to get it out my pocket. *Please let it be Grandma Stephy. Please. Please. Please.*

"Thank God," I say aloud when I see her name flash across the screen. I press talk and put the phone to my ear.

"What the hell did they do to you?" she asks before I can even say hello.

I briefly contemplate telling her I'll talk to her when I get to her house, when I'm not around Kyler, but then she announces she's out of town on a trip with Harry.

"Don't worry, though, hon. After I got your message, I hopped in the car, and I'm headed straight to the airport. Harry's on his phone right now, looking for a flight home." Anger fills her tone. "Goddamn those two. I can't believe they're doing this to you."

"Me, either." But as soon as I say it, I know it's a lie. I'm not surprised this is happening. In fact, when I look back at my relationship with my dad and Lynn, I'm surprised they didn't try to send me away sooner.

Tears well in my eyes as every painful memory and hurtful word comes rushing back to me. Suddenly, everything pours out of me in a jumble. I tell Grandma Stephy about how Lynn said my mom was dead and that she was a bad person, how I pushed Lynn and ran out of the house, how they'll call the cops on me if I don't go to Montana. By the time I'm finished babbling, I'm out of breath and highly aware that Kyler is watching me out of the corner of his eye.

"Damn my son and that stupid bitch he calls his wife,"

she says when I'm finished. "I'm not going to let them do this to you. They're not sending you anywhere. You're going to stay with me."

"But what if they call the cops?" I turn toward the window, not wanting to see the look on Kyler's face right now. If he didn't think I was a freak before, he probably does now. "What if they call me in as a runaway?"

"I highly doubt it." She seems pretty confident. "Lynn is all about appearances. That's probably part of the reason she took you in as her own daughter—to cover up your father's affair. I'm going to call your father and make sure his stupid ass doesn't let her."

"What should I do until then?" I ask, dabbing my eyes with the sleeve of my jacket.

"Where are you right now?"

"Um..." I sneak a peek in Kyler's direction. He's fiddling with the stereo, pretending to be oblivious to this crazy conversation going on right beside him. "Um, I'm actually with Kyler right now. Kyler Meyers. You baked cookies for him that one time."

"Oh, that boy you've been in love with forever," she says way too loudly.

My gaze flits to Kyler again, wondering if he heard what she just said. His hands are on the wheel, his focus straight ahead on the road, but I swear the corners of his lips twitch.

"No... I mean, yeah, that's him. But I'm not..." I bite

down on my tongue to stop myself from saying anything embarrassing. Anything else, anyway.

"All right, I'll let you off the hook. But when I get home, I want the details," she teases me. "Can he take you to my house?"

"We're already heading there," I say, resting my head against the window.

"Good. There's a spare key under the welcome mat. Indigo will be there around ten, but send her a text to let her know you're there so she'll come straight home."

"What about Lynn and my dad?" I ask. "What if they show up there?"

"You let me handle them." The way she says it causes me to shudder. I love my Grandma Stephy to death, but I pity the person who makes an enemy of her.

There was this one time she kept getting into an argument with one of her neighbors about the height of the shrubs in her yard. He kept threatening to call the police, saying they were hideous to look at and needed to be short enough that they were out of sight.

When he finally made an official complaint, she cut down her shrubs and then, in the middle of the night, snuck into his yard and whacked down all of the guy's prize roses. The dude was obsessed with his roses to the point where he would spend all weekend attending to them.

After she destroyed them, she piled both her shrubs

and the roses into a barrel, put them in the middle of his yard and lit them on fire. He came running out of his house, freaking out, and all my grandma said was, "There you go. Now both our problems are solved. You don't have to look at my shrubs anymore, and I don't have to witness you fondling your rose bushes."

The man went livid and called the cops on her. The police wrote her up, but I think they thought it was funny, because they kept cracking jokes about rose bush fetishes as they took down notes.

"You'll call me after you talk to them, though, right?" I ask her.

"Of course," she promises. "Give me a few and I'll call you right back."

After we say goodbye, I hang up and put my phone away. Then I remain quiet, unsure of what to say to Kyler. I kind of just want to remain that way for the rest of the drive to avoid telling him anything, but Kyler decides to break the silence.

"I've always known Lynn was a bitch to you, but I didn't know she was that bad." His grip tightens on the steering wheel as he casts a glance at me. "Isa, I'm so sorry you had to go through all that."

I shrug, acting all blasé, even though on the inside, I'm a bundle of bouncy, hyped-up-on-sugar monkeys. "It's not your fault."

"I know, but…" A deafening breath puffs from his lips.

"About what Hannah said earlier, I want to be truthful with you, okay?"

Whoa. So, we're going there. *Now* of all times.

"I just want you to know I've never called you a loser." He pauses and I start to thank him, but then he adds, "But."

The cringe-worthy *but*, the word people use before they say something you might not want to hear.

"I never really tried to stop people when they said stuff about you." His voice is soft, conveying shame.

I'm not sure what to say. Part of my infatuation with Kyler came from the fact that I thought he stuck up for me, like when Hannah was teasing me and he stepped in. Or when his friends cornered me in the school, and he got them to leave me alone by telling them they were late for practice. Secretly, I always pictured him as this knight in shining armor who forced everyone to stop making fun of me even when I wasn't around to hear it.

"Isa." His cautious tone makes me apprehensive. "I've done some things in my past I'm not proud of, but I want you to know I'm not like that anymore."

Since when? Since I came back from Europe with my makeover? Since I became, as Indigo put it, "smokin' hot"? I want to ask him, but I'm afraid I'll have to watch him squirm in the seat and struggle for an answer, that his reaction will crush the last five years I spent dreaming of being with him one day. It was those dreams—fantasizing about another life—that got me through some of my roughest days of high school. I always convinced myself that I'd one day change. Everyone would see it—Kyler would see it—and my life would get better.

But now I'm sitting here with him, completely changed, yet my life is falling apart.

"I sometimes used to watch you when you were out on your balcony, drawing," he confesses. "You always looked so into it. I envied the way you could tune everything out like that. I've always had a really hard time not giving a shit about what people were doing, thinking, saying."

"I wasn't always focused on my drawing," I admit. On the inside, though, I'm like *holy cupids and chocolate hearts, Kyler used to watch me like I did him?* "Sometimes, I just pretended I was when... when I was worried you might see me."

A smile breaks out across his face. "So, you watched me too?"

I roll my eyes. "You know I did."

"No, I didn't," he tries to lie, but when I blast him with a skeptical look, he caves. "Okay. Okay. I did know, but I liked knowing you did. It made me feel..." He wavers. "Special, I guess."

A laugh bursts from my lips, and I slap my hand across my mouth. "I'm so sorry. I didn't mean to laugh. You just said special, and it sounded so..."

"So what?" he presses. When I shake my head, he reaches over and tickles my leg. "Come on. You can't laugh at a guy like that and not explain why."

I do one of my infamous pig snorts. "Kyler, stop!" I cry through my laughter.

"Not until you tell me why you laughed." His fingers lightly trace over my leg until I finally throw my hands in the air, surrendering.

"Fine. I laughed because it sounded like a line from a cheesy romantic movie." I wipe the tears of laughter from my eyes.

"It kind of did, didn't it?" His lips pull into a grin. "You're really cute when you laugh that hard, especially with the whole pig snort thing. That was super attractive."

I playfully swat his arm. "Whatever. I love my pig snort."

"So do I," he says, sounding genuine. "It's so real. A lot of girls do that whole high-pitched fake laugh."

I know what kind of laugh he's talking about because Hannah does it all the time.

An extremely intense look crosses his face. I have no clue what he's about to say, but I hold my breath in anticipation. Before he gets a chance to say anything, though, my phone chirps and ruins the moment.

"It's my grandma," I say then answer it.

"Okay, I've got everything taken care of," she says in a rush. "For now, you'll be staying with me."

"For now?" I ask, panicking. "Does that mean I'll eventually have to go back?"

"No, that means that, for now, your dad's agreed to let you stay with me until things have cooled off," she explains. "I'm going to have to fight him, though, once Lynn gets involved. I can already tell that. But I will fight it. I'm not letting you go back to that house. I need you to do something for me, though. I need you to be on your best behavior. The last thing we need right now is to give them anything that they can use against us."

I'm worried about what this will do to her health. "Are you sure you want to do this? I don't want to stress you out or anything."

"Stressed out? It'll be a relief to know you're away from all that shit," she replies matter-of-factly. "I've spent so many nights worrying if you're okay."

"What if they call the cops and report me as a runaway or something?" I ask. "I don't want to get you into trouble."

"They're not going to call the cops," she insists. "They may have threatened you with that, but I have a feeling, if they did, they'd end up in more trouble than you would."

A weight falls off my shoulders, but I have to wonder... "Why would they get into trouble?"

"Lots of reasons, hon', like if I reported them as

neglectful, abusive parents. And you told me she grabbed you, right?"

"It's not that bad," I say quietly, wrapping my fingers around my wrist.

"I don't care if it's bad. She has no right to grab you like that," she says. "Plus, there's that whole thing with your dad's company."

Huh? "What're you talking about? What's going on with my dad's company?"

"Nothing that you should worry about," she replies hastily. "Look, I have to go. I'm getting ready to go through security. I should be home around eleven or so, and then we'll talk more. And I don't want you sitting around and stressing out about stuff. Go out and do something. Maybe you could ask that Kyler boy to take you to a movie or something. I bet that'd be a *great* distraction."

I resist the urge to cover the phone. Kyler's probably already heard everything she's said, anyway.

After I hang up, Kyler confirms my suspicions when he turns to me and says, "She wants me to take you to a movie, huh?"

I feel my cheeks warm. "You don't have to. She just doesn't want me sitting around at the house by myself. I'll be fine, though. Sometimes, I think she still thinks of me as a little kid who needs to be watched 24/7."

"I'm sure she's just worried about you." He presses on

the brakes, stopping at a red light. "I don't blame her. It has to be hard, dealing with parents like that."

"It is, but I'm used to it." I shrug, like *What're you going to do? Life's life, man.*

He considers something while studying me. He keeps his eyes on me until the light turns green, and then he flips on his blinker and veers left, breaking about five traffic laws.

"I'm not going to let you sit around by yourself all day." He steers the car down a road that leads toward the center of Sunnyvale. "I'll keep you distracted until your grandma comes home."

I glance at the clock on the dash. "But that's not for, like, eight hours."

He arches a brow. "You don't think I can distract you for eight hours?"

I keep my mouth shut, refusing to say what runs through my head: *Maybe if you took your shirt off.* Instead, I say, and might I add, awesomely calmly, "What're we going to do?"

His eyes sparkle mischievously. "I have an idea."

"Okay." I'm a little nervous, but curiosity gets the better of me. "What's your idea?"

He stops the car in front of the park right by the court then silences the engine. "A game of horse."

"That sounds fun." I unbuckle my seatbelt. "But I'm

not sure even you can make a game of horse last eight hours."

"Oh, that's just the start of the distraction." He grins wickedly. "I'm going to make a little game out of it."

I smirk at him. "Um, you do realize horse is a game, right?"

He counters with a dirty look. "That's not what I meant."

I can't help giggling. "Then what did you mean?"

He slides the keys out of the ignition. "For every game I win, I get to pick something crazy we both have to do. And for every game you win, you get to pick something."

"You do realize I rock at horse, right? And I've kicked your ass at it before."

"I've gotten a little bit better since I was twelve." He reaches for the door handle, flashing me a cocky smile. "But if you're too afraid of getting your butt kicked, we can do something else."

I kind of want to hug him right now because I'm smiling and hardly thinking about Lynn, my dad, and how awful it'll be if they end up sending me to Montana.

"Game on, dude." I comb my fingers through my hair as I catch sight of my reflection in the mirror. Ugh. I haven't had a chance to clean myself up since the whole meltdown thing yesterday. Between the smeared eyeliner and the runny mascara, I look like I'm trying to go goth. "Just one sec."

I retrieve my brush from my bag and pull my hair into a ponytail as he gets out of the car and grabs a basketball from the trunk. I use one of my shirts to wipe the day old makeup off my face. I consider reapplying it, but I don't want to make Kyler wait on me. It's been a while since I've gone this natural, and I'll admit I feel a bit self-conscious. Still, I hold my head high as I get out of the car and hike toward the courts with Kyler. I'm not going to feel bad for being me and looking like me. I've already spent too many days feeling like that.

As we near the edge of the grass, Kyler inches toward me. "You have the cutest freckles." He brushes his fingers across my cheek. "I've always thought that."

I have to remind myself to breathe. With the way he touched me, so intimately, I'm not sure how to react. It's strange that the thing he thinks is cute about me is the thing I've been covering up with makeup.

I'm not sure what to make of what's going on between us, but I definitely smile. The smile vanishes, though, when I notice a dark blue car with tinted windows driving by the park at an exceedingly sluggish pace.

At first, I don't pay too much attention to it, but as it rounds the park for the third time, almost slowing to stop beside the courts, unease stirs inside me. What if it's someone looking for me? Like maybe my parents? It's not their car, but I wouldn't put it past them to borrow one just to surprise attack me. Or could it be an unmarked police vehicle?

"What are you staring at?" Kyler asks as he jogs across the court, going in for a slam-dunk.

"I…" I peek back to the where the car was, only to find it speeding off toward the main road. "There was this car driving around, but I guess it was nothing."

He dribbles the ball, his brows knitting. "Do you think it was your parents?"

"No, I don't think so… It wasn't their car, and I don't think they'd look for me here." They don't know me well enough to.

I shrug the uneasiness off the best I can and raise my hands in front of me, focusing on the game. Still, something doesn't quite feel right, like the calm before a storm. I just wish I knew what kind of storm was coming.

5

KAI

"A THOUSAND BUCKS? A *THOUSAND BUCKS*?" BIG DOUG repeats the same thing over and over again with a look of astonishment on his face. Finally, he sits down in the chair in front of his cluttered desk, his eyes wide as he shakes his head. "Kai, how the fuck did you end up in this mess? I thought you were being more careful."

"I was being careful." I sink down in a folding chair. "But then I vouched for Bradon even though he has a shitty rep. I figured, since he was my friend, he wouldn't screw me over."

Big Doug reaches for a bag of opened chips propped against one of his multiple computers. "Dude, Bradon screws everyone over, friend or not."

I lower my head into my hands. "I'm realizing that now."

"You're too nice, man."

"Is there such a thing?"

"Um, yeah. When you try to help people you know are going to get you into trouble, that's called being too nice."

"All right, I get it. I made a bad decision. Tell me something I don't know." I raise my head. "But I need to focus on fixing the problem. What's done is done, and now I need to come up with a thousand bucks before I get my ass kicked. T plays dirty. He'll probably get a bunch of his buddies to jump me. He won't give a shit if it isn't a fair fight."

He munches on a handful of chips. "I have a couple of small jobs I need done. It won't get you a thousand, but it's a start."

I wish I had a better solution, but right now, Big Doug's offer is the only thing I've got. "I'll take whatever I can get."

"Okay, let's get you started." He spins the chair around, facing the largest computer screen. "I have to ask, though, why not just ask your parents for the money?"

"They wouldn't give it to me, even if I did ask," I mutter, rubbing the heels of my hands against my eyes. This shit's giving me a headache, but it's mild in comparison to what would happen if I don't come up with the cash.

The keys click as he taps his fingers against them.

"Even if you explain the situation to them? Maybe you could tell them the truth. I mean, I know it's not ideal, but I'm sure they'd rather help you than see you get hurt."

I refuse to feel the wave of hurt washing over me. "Trust me. My father wouldn't care. He'd probably tell me that I deserved whatever was coming for me."

I can hear him now. *"You got yourself into this mess, so you can get yourself out of it. It's not my problem. You're not my problem."* He's right, too. This is all my fault. Every dumbass choice I've made has led me to this point in my life.

I force thoughts of my dad's disappointment out of my head. "What exactly are these jobs?"

"The first one's pretty simple." He clicks the mouse a few times, opening multiple programs. "I just need you to deliver something for me."

"That doesn't sound too bad."

"It doesn't sound bad, but this delivery is super fucking important. You can't mess it up at all, okay, man?" he says and I nod. "It pays a hundred bucks, and gas is included."

"Gas?" I rise to my feet as the printer turns on. "How far am I driving?"

He wheels the chair over to the printer. "To Mapleview."

"But that's, like, a two-hour drive each way." I run my hand over my head as I pace the length of his basement.

Normally, I wouldn't give a shit about taking a four-hour drive, but with everything going on with Isa, I want to be close in case she needs me. She hasn't called yet, and she promised me she'd call after she was done talking to her dad.

"If it's too far, I can get someone else to do it." His tone implies I should keep my mouth shut and be grateful he's doing me a favor.

"No, I'm good. I just needed to do something, but it can wait, I guess." I take my phone out of my back pocket and check my messages.

Nothing.

I decide to message her to see if she's okay.

Me: Hey, just wanted to make sure everything is okay. You never called me, but maybe you're still talking to your dad. I'm actually headed out of town for the day, but I'll be back later today.

Isa: Oh, my God! Sorry I forgot to call you! All crap hit the fan when I went home, and I completely forgot! I'm okay. I'm not even at the house right now. I ran out after Lynn threatened to send me to some reform school in Montana. I'm actually going to be staying with Grandma Stephy for a little bit until we can figure out what to do, but she promised me she wouldn't let them send me away.

Anger simmers inside me. Dammit. Her parents are such assholes.

Me: WTF??? They're trying to send you away to Montana? What the hell is wrong with them?

Isa: Well, Lynn said it was because of my violence problem because, apparently, pushing her once means I have a violence problem. But honestly, I have a feeling she's been planning this for a while. She had all these papers printed out, and she was all ready to ship me off tomorrow morning.

Me: God, I hate that woman... What did your dad say?

Isa: The usual, that he agrees with Lynn. I'm not surprised. He always agrees with Lynn when it comes to me. I'm guessing it's because he feels guilty I'm the product of an affair.

Me: I don't care if he feels guilty or not. He's your dad, and he needs to act like one.

Isa: I wish he did, but I honestly don't think he ever will. I'm starting to make peace with that, though. I'm just lucky I have my grandma Stephy. She's practically like a mom and dad to me. I don't know what I'd do without her. And Indigo, too.

Me: You know I'm here for you if you need anything.

Isa: I know. You've really been awesome to me lately, Kai. I appreciate it. I really do.

I want to be there for her today. After what happened

with her parents, I'm betting she could use someone to talk to.

Me: Are you with your grandma now?

Isa: No. She's actually out of town, but she's flying in tonight.

There's no way she should be alone right now.

Me: Want to take a little drive to Mapleview? I could use a driving buddy.

It takes her a minute to answer, and the moment the message buzzes through, I know I'm not going to like her answer.

Isa: I'm with Kyler right now. We're supposed to hang out until my grandma gets home. Why are you going to Mapleview? If you need me to go with you, I totally will, especially if you want to talk about whatever's going on with you and that T guy.

I open and flex my fingers. She's with Kyler? What the hell? Did he just wait around the house so he was there to jump in when Isa needed rescuing then cleared his entire schedule? I know for a fact that he had plans later today after he took Isa to breakfast. I heard him talking about it with his friends on the phone after Isa left our house, saying something about needing to get some practice hours in.

Me: Nah. It's okay. I think I'm just going to ask Big Doug to drive with me.

It's a complete lie. Yeah, it hurts like a bitch to think

about her and Kyler hanging out, doing God knows what, but I don't want her to come with me just because she feels sorry for me. I've had too many girls do that—hang out with me because they felt bad for using me to get to Kyler.

Isa: Okay... If you change your mind, let me know. I think we should definitely talk about what's going on with you. Can we hang out tomorrow?

Me: Yeah. Maybe. I'll text you later and let you know.

I leave it at that and put my phone away, trying not to think about what she and Kyler could be doing. But it's all I think about. Fuck, I have way too vivid an imagination. Seriously. I swear my mind's trying to torture me to death with images of Isa and Kyler and what they could be doing.

"So, who is she?" Big Doug's question rips through my thoughts.

"Huh?" I take the manila envelope he's holding out to me.

"The girl who's got you all worked up," he says, swiveling the chair around. "You look like you're about to lose your shit."

"No, I don't." Stamped across the top of the envelope in bright red letters are the words DO NOT OPEN along with a smiley face sticker. "What's with you and these stickers? You put them on everything."

"They're my mark," he answers simply. "It lets people know where I've been and what work is mine. I don't want other people taking credit for my shit."

I give the envelope a shake, noting it feels really light. "What's in this?"

"Don't worry about that." He waves me off then continues on with his questioning. "Is it that girl from the party? The one who needed me to find info on her mom?" When I reluctantly nod, he adds, "How'd she take the news about her mom?"

I tuck the envelope under my arm. "I haven't told her yet."

He blinks at me in shock. "Why the hell not?"

"I was planning on it, but then some shit happened with her family... I'm worried she might not be able to handle it right now."

"It doesn't matter what you think. She deserves to know, and the longer you sit on this, the more pissed she's going to be when you do tell her."

"I know." I crack my knuckles as his words sink in. He's right. Even if Isa is going through a ton of family drama right now, I need to tell her as soon as I can. "Dude, you're starting to sound like Dr. Phil."

Big Doug tucks his arms behind his head. "I watch that show all the time."

I give him a *really* look. "Are you being serious?"

"What? I got nothing better to do between jobs.

Besides, I learn a lot from it, like when to tell a girl you're obsessed with that you know something about her family. Something, I might add, that she asked for help with."

"All right. I get it. I'll tell her. Just stop Psych 101-ing me and drop it."

He holds up a finger. "One more thing." He opens a drawer to a filing cabinet, collects a folder with a smiley face sticker on it, and hands it to me. "I felt bad about being the bearer of such fucked-up news, so I decided to do some more research on this Bella woman and found out more about her case."

"What'd you find out?" Considering Big Doug rarely does favors for people, I'm shocked he did this.

"Some pretty interesting stuff. I'm actually kind of surprised the woman was found guilty. Then again, some of the stuff I pulled up wasn't used in the case and isn't accessible to the public. She filed for an appeal a couple of times, and I think her most recent one got approved, but it might take a while for anything to happen. I'm still looking into a few more things, but I thought I'd give this to you for now. It might give Isa a little bit of peace of mind until I can find out more."

"Wait. Did you hack into the case records or something?" I peek into the folder and cringe as I skim over the top page.

Before I can get too far into it, he slams his hand

down on top of the folder, closing it. "You can look at that later. Right now, we work."

Then he jumps right in and gives me a list of instructions to follow when I deliver the package. After hearing the list, I realize it is a bigger job than I originally thought, and I feel even more uneasy about what the hell's in the envelope.

1. Under no circumstances am I to look into the envelope.
2. Before I pull up to the set location, I'm to drive around the block three times.
3. If I see anyone who looks even a bit suspicious, I'm supposed to drive off and head home without dropping off the envelope.
4. Keep my car door locked at all times. Even when the guy comes to pick up the envelope, I'm only supposed to crack the window and slip it through.
5. The guy picking it up will be wearing a hoodie and brass knuckles.
6. The second I give the guy the envelope, I need to leave Mapleview. But don't drive straight home. I need to cruise on the back roads for about an hour before getting on the highway.
7. I can't take my cell phone with me.

"What?" I say after he rattles off number seven. "Why the heck not?"

"For tracking purposes." He sticks out his hand. "Hand it over, man."

I retrieve my phone from my back pocket, but don't hand it over. "Just a second." I hurriedly type a quick text to Isa, deciding it's time to tell her.

Me: Yeah, let's definitely get together tomorrow. Just let me know what time to pick you up.

Before I receive a response, Big Doug snatches the phone from my hand.

"Dude, give me that back," I gripe, reaching to take it back.

He spins the chair around, shoves my phone into a desk drawer, and then locks it away. "I'll give it back to you when the job's done. And the hundred bucks."

When I hear my phone vibrate inside the drawer, I grind my teeth. "Just let me check that."

He shakes his head. "You have the envelope. You're officially on the clock."

I consider telling him to fuck off but stop myself since he's doing me a huge favor.

"See you in five hours." He starts the timer on a computer.

Sighing, I turn toward the door, feeling unsettled about what I'm about to do. Yeah, I've done some shady things over the last year. I've broken into cars, partied, done some illegal stuff like helping hack into security systems, bought weed off T and dealt for him a couple of times. The whole drug thing was a little too intense for me, though. I was nervous and panicky making the drops, and I quickly stopped both buying and selling. When Bradon tracked me down at a party, it'd been months since I had seen T.

"I need a favor," he said, nervously glancing around at the people drinking and smoking around us. He was so twitchy I wondered if he was on something.

At first, I just shook my head. A favor for Bradon usually meant trouble.

But then he begged and pleaded. "Please, Kai. My family's in some serious financial trouble, and I need the money, like, really bad, or we're gonna lose everything."

He looked upset, and I started to feel sorry for him.

"What'd you need?" I asked.

"For you to vouch to T for me," he said quickly. "Just tell him that he can trust me."

"Can he?" I question because Bradon was never the trustworthy type. He was either stealing from people or stealing and lying about it.

"I won't screw you over," he promised. "I just need to do a couple of jobs for him so I can earn some cash fast. But he needs someone he knows—like you—to vouch for me."

Every one of my instincts screamed at me not to do

this, that Bradon was going to end up screwing me over, but then he gave me this whole speech about his family losing their house and car, and I caved like a sucker.

In the end, Bradon ended up selling the drugs for T and never giving him any of the money. At first, I didn't get too pissed off, because I thought maybe he did it in a panic move to bail his family out of their financial trouble. But a couple of days ago, I found out that was all a lie.

Bradon has gotten into some pretty hardcore drugs and needed quick cash to feed his addiction. From what I understand, his parents gave him an intervention yesterday, and he took off to rehab. I feel like an idiot for believing his sob story and not seeing his drug problem had gotten that out of hand. But there's nothing I can do about it now. T warned me that, if Bradon screwed him over, his debt would fall on me.

I just hope whatever I'm about to do isn't going to end with me being in even more trouble.

6

ISABELLA

I DRIBBLE THE BALL AGAINST THE CONCRETE AS I calculate where to make my next shot. So far, Kyler and I are both tied at HORS. It's taken us over an hour just to get to that point because we both rock at the game and rarely miss a basket. It's fun spending time with him. What's really cool is that he hasn't brought up my mom and dad. While I know I'm eventually going to have to talk about it, it's nice to take a break from the emotional chaos.

"Quit procrastinating losing," Kyler taunts as he watches me walk the length of the court.

I stop near the half court and smile sweetly at him. "You mean, you losing?"

He chuckles, fishing out his phone from his pocket.

"In your dreams. And when I win, you owe me," he says, reading a text.

"You're so not going to win. And you want to know why?" I raise my arms with the ball in my hands.

He leans against the pole of the hoop, folding his arms, amusement dancing in his eyes. "Because you're so awesome?"

"Yep." Grinning, I take the shot. From out of my peripheral vision, I swear I see a flash, like a camera, and I wonder if it might be Kyler, but when I look at him again, I don't see his phone in his hand. And why would he take a photo of me?

Shoving the weird paranoia aside, I watch the ball soar through the air, swish through the basket, and I break out in a goofy dance, throwing my hands in the air and tapping my feet.

Kyler laughs as he chases down the ball. "Cute victory dance, but FYI, you haven't won yet." With that, he strolls up to where I'm standing and easily makes the basket.

I stop dancing, gather the ball in my hands, and inch back farther to make a shot. But I try to go too big and end up missing. Now Kyler's the one to dance around like he's already won.

I can't help giggling at his silly dance moves. "You still haven't won."

"I've got this in the bag now." He appears pretty confident as he strides around behind me and presses his solid chest against my back. My breath gets caught in my throat as my heart dang near explodes out of my chest. My body shakes from the sensation, and I quickly step forward before he notices.

But his fingers fold around my arm and draw me back against him. "Nope. You need to stay put for this one." He lets go of my arm and rests his elbows on my shoulder.

After he shoots the basket, I spin around and put my hands on my hips, giving him the death glare. "No fair."

"Why isn't that fair?" he asks innocently.

"Um, hello, because you're, like, five inches taller than me." Sure, I'm not short or anything, but Kyler is tall. For me to be able to even get my elbows onto his shoulders, I'd have to get a stepstool.

"I'll tell you what." He's totally enjoying this. "I'll make it easy on you. Just make the shot from here."

Like hell I'm taking the easy way out.

I square my shoulders. "No way. I'm *going* to win this fair and square." I skip around him. Then, with a jump, I hurry and rest my elbows on his shoulders for a split second, quickly tossing the ball. It arches through the air, and at first I think it's going to make it, but at the last second, it curves left, dings the rim, and falls to the ground. "Mother of all zombies."

Kyler whirls around with a ha-ha-I-just-kicked-your-behind look on his face. "You should've taken the easy shot."

"No way." I grimace, partly joking but partly not because, man, I hate losing! "It wouldn't have felt like a real win."

"But now I win." His grin is as shiny as a disco ball.

I want to sulk and be a sore loser, but he looks too adorable standing there shirtless with his hair a tousled mess and his skin lightly damp with sweat. "Fine. What crazy thing are we doing?"

"Aw, don't pout." He lightly prods me with his elbow. "I promise I'll pick something fun."

I frown for two point five more seconds before the smile wins. "Fine. What're we doing?" I bounce on my toes, bursting with anticipation.

He laughs, his eyes crinkling at the corners. "I think that might be the quickest I've ever seen anyone get over losing."

I rub the light sheen of sweat from my hairline with the back of my hand. "What can I say? I'm a sucker for surprises." I clasp my hands together. "Now please, pretty please, tell me what we're doing."

He shakes his head, scooping up the ball. "No way. It won't be a surprise if I tell you."

I follow after him as he starts across the grass toward the car. "Oh, come on." I grasp his arm. "We never agreed it had to be a surprise, just that the winner got to pick something crazy that we'd both have to do."

He digs his car keys from his pocket. "Yeah, but I think it's more fun this way."

I jut out my bottom lip. "Says who?"

"Says me." His gaze briefly falls to my fingers on his arm.

All of my insecurities overwhelm me, and I pull away from him, my cheeks warming.

A beat or two skips by, and the silence makes my cheeks heat even more with embarrassment. Trying to chill out, I focus on everything else except Kyler staring at me: the leaves gusting across the dry grass, a horn honking in the distance, the playground swings squeaking against the wind, the tree Kai and I used to hide in when we were younger and just a couple of days ago during lunch when we almost kissed, and a twenty-something-year-old guy with dark brown hair, leaning against a tree, watching us as like a creeper.

What the hell? Maybe he was the one who took a photo of me when I made the shot. But why? That doesn't make any sense.

Stop worrying so much, Isa. No one wants a photo of you.

When the guy notices me observing him, he waves sheepishly before jogging toward the parking lot and across the street, disappearing into a nearby neighborhood.

I'm not sure what to make of it or if I should make anything of it.

Just chill, dude. You seriously watch too many horror movies.

"I think you're adorable." Kyler tucks a strand of my hair behind my ear, drawing my attention back to him. "You get so excited over the simplest things. It's such a nice break from what I'm used to."

"You know, that's the second time you've mentioned I'm a nice break from what you're used to." I cringe at the breathlessness in my voice.

"I know." His voice is soft and his eyes are on mine as his tongue slips out of his mouth and wets his lips. Then his gaze drops to my mouth.

Wow, wow, wow … in my wildest dreams … Is he going to kiss me? is the first thought that races through my mind, but then it's followed by hesitancy. Is this really how I want the kiss to go down? On the day my parents threatened to send me off to reform school? Wouldn't that make the memory of it tainted?

I shove the thought aside, though, when my stomach does a kick flip. No, I want this kiss. Who cares if this morning was crappy? I can erase the crappy and replace it with *fireworks. Fireworks, everywhere.*

I barely breathe as I wait for him to kiss me, my heart shape-shifting into a freakin' hummingbird, fluttering a million miles a minute.

But he suddenly hesitates, raking his fingers through his hair as he stares at the street. "Isa, I want to get to know you more. In the past, I've never taken the time to get to know the girls I've gone out with. But I want things to be different with you. I want to take my time and enjoy every moment."

A couple things cross my mind at the moment: 1). Does he mean he wants to get to know me as a friend? 2) He's obviously working on reinventing himself, but why? Where did the sudden change come from? Because there's usually a reason behind someone wanting to change, like me, like Kai, even though I still have no clue why he went from popular, preppy guy to bad boy in the span of a night.

I want to ask Kyler if something's going on with him, but I chicken out. "Okay."

He looks at me again, smiling as he threads his fingers through mine and pulls me toward the car.

I feel the slightest bit of excitement from his touch but a drop of disappointment at the same time. I don't know why. Is it just lingering sensations of the almost kiss? Or something else?

"Ready for crazy task number one?" he asks, squeezing my hand.

I nod, tearing my thoughts from my worries. Nope, I'm not supposed to be worrying about stuff today, whether it's my parents, my mom, or what's going on with Kyler. Today is supposed to be about being distracted from the craziness in my life, and I'll be damned if I'm going to go into worrying-about-a-guy mode. I'm going to focus on whatever Kyler's got in store for me and nothing else.

7

ISABELLA

"Um…" I'm unsure what to say to the scene in front of me.

Kyler said it was a surprise, and while I wasn't sure what to expect, I wasn't expecting this.

"I promise it'll be fun." He reaches over the console, brushes my ponytail off my shoulder, and gently massages my shoulder. "And it's an excellent distraction."

My muscle tense from his touch, mostly because I'm not used to being touched so much. But he doesn't seem to notice, his fingertips delicately kneading my muscles.

I concentrate on the football field we're parked by. A bunch of guys are on the field, throwing and catching the ball, and several girls a year or two older than me are watching from the benches. I've seen a couple of the girls at the parties Hannah's thrown at our house, and most of the guys are Kyler's friends from high school. Nausea forms in the pit of my stomach when I realize a few of them have made fun of me at one point or another.

"None of the girls are playing."

A challenge glimmers in his eyes. "I didn't think you were the kind of girl who cared about stuff like that."

"I'm not." It's the truth. I just used the girls not playing as an excuse to avoid telling him the real reason I don't want to play flag football with a bunch of dudes—because I'd rather spend time locked in a dungeon than play football with his friends who can be total douchebags.

I rack my brain for a legit sounding excuse, but all that pops into my mind is, *Sorry, can't. I'm allergic to football and all balls in general. Yep, sounds super legit, Isa. Face palm.*

"Look, I know you said you thought football was kind of boring, but I really think, if you try to play it, you might like it," he says. "Besides, it might get your mind off other stuff."

He has a point, but paintballing or playing video games would do that for me, too, and I wouldn't have to hang out with a group of people who spent years bullying me.

"No one's going to say anything to you," he adds, as if reading my mind. "I promise."

I give him a fake smile, wondering if he can tell it's

forced. "Okay. Yeah. Sure. Just give me a second. I need to make a call first."

"You want me to wait for you?"

"Nah. It might take a minute."

He nods and hops out of the car. Once he shuts the door, I punch in Indigo's number. She doesn't answer, so I text her to call me ASAP, saying I need a ride. I give her exactly one minute to respond before I panic and dial Kai's number. I know he said he was going to Mapleview, but I'm hoping upon hope that he ended up not going. He never did text me back, though, when I replied to his message about hanging out tomorrow. I told him sure and asked where he wanted to meet. Maybe he never replied because he didn't have a signal. The drive to Mapleview is pretty much a dead zone.

After four rings, his phone goes to voicemail.

"Hey, it's me... Isa..." I'm unsure if I should tell him what's going on. "Look, I'm kind of in a mess and really need a ride. I know you said you were leaving town, but I'm hoping maybe you haven't left yet... But anyway, yeah, I'm guessing you have; otherwise, you probably would've answered your phone." I hang up, shaking my head at my rambling message.

I don't get out of the car right away. Instead, I sit in the car and watch Kyler and his friends from out the window. I know I'm being a coward, but I feel like a mouse about to walk into a lion's den. I have no idea why

Kyler would bring me here when he knows how much his and Hannah's friends despise me. Could that be the point? Perhaps this is some trap Hannah's set up. Maybe, when I get out of the car, she'll step out from underneath the bleachers, and she and her ra-ra space cadets will break out in a chorus of "Isabella Smellera."

After a few minutes tick by, I decide it's time to face the inevitable. I grab the door handle and open the door. Part of me wants to flee in the opposite direction and run down the road. I honestly might have if Kyler didn't spot me. He waves me over with a smile on his face, and all of his friends stare at me.

Cringe. Cringe. Double cringe.

Why couldn't I have just taken the easy shot during horse?

I bump the door shut, zip my jacket up, and keep my head down as I hike across the field toward them. It feels like the first day of school after I got back from my trip, all made over, a completely different person on the outside. Still, I hardly looked up at anyone as I walked, too afraid they'd still see me as Hannah's dorky younger sister.

But I'm not Hannah's dorky younger sister. I never really was. Hannah and Lynn just made me believe that. But if I look down at the ground right now, then I kind of am, aren't I?

Sucking in a deep breath, I level my gaze on Kyler. I'm not sure what he told his friends about why I'm here, but none of them seem that interested in me. The guys go back to warming up, and most of the girls go back to chatting with each other. But a couple of them have their gazes locked on me like they're ready to swoop in and attack.

"So, when you said come play flag football, did you actually mean I had to play?" I ask Kyler, coming to stop in front of him.

He thrums his finger against his lips. "What do you think?"

"I don't know. I'm kind of hoping you just meant you'd teach me how to throw a ball." I give him my best hopeful look.

He chucks the ball in the air, giving me a lopsided grin. "Come on, Isa. I thought we talked about this." He catches the ball and grips it in his hand. "That you were going to be different than them." He nods his chin over at the girls then waggles his brows. "You know you wanna."

If it were any other sport, I'd be all over this, but I know zilch about football. "All right, but you're going to have to show me a couple of things first." I put my hands together and bow to him. "Oh, great one, please show me your knowledge."

He chuckles, but I can tell my remark goes way over his head. Huh. Guess it only works with Kai. "Okay, we'll practice catching first."

For the next twenty minutes, Kyler does just that. He's passionate about it, too. While he looks super cute with his eyes lit up with excitement, I find myself getting kind of bored. Still, I act like a good pupil and pay attention even when my stomach grumbles in hunger. I tell it to shut its trap, that food will come later, but then a guy walks by, munching on a cup of ice cream. It looks like strawberry, too, with cheesecake bits.

Man, I'm so hungry even vegetables are starting to sound good.

"We'll get something to eat after the game," Kyler tells me, rotating the football in his hands.

Um... Did I just say that aloud?

"Okay." I resist the urge to take the damn ball from him, toss it into the tree, and declare the game over.... Hmm... Kai said I was like a gremlin when I get hungry. I guess he was right.

Kyler spends another couple of minutes making me catch the ball before he deems me ready to play. He and a guy I'm guessing Kyler knows from college, because he looks older, get voted captains. I quickly find out his name is Wes and that he's kind of a sexist asshole.

"If she's going to play," Wes says to Kyler while pointing a finger at me, "another girl's going to have to, too, so the teams will be fair."

"Why? Isa's more athletic than Ben and Tim," Kyler replies, tucking a ball under his arm. "In fact, she might be better than you." He winks at me.

Pride swells in my chest as I smile at Wes. *Yeah, dude, just because you have a penis, it doesn't mean you're the shit.*

Wes rolls his eyes. "Whatever, man. You're so just trying to get laid right now."

A few of the guys snicker, but Kyler shoves Wes, and kind of hard, too.

"Shut up," he warns, glaring at Wes. "You're such a prick sometimes."

I look away as I feel my cheeks flame. Oh, my God, I'm so uncomfortable right now. Maybe I should just bail out and chase Ice Cream Dude down. I could be all like, "Hand over the ice cream, or else a murderous, man-eating monster will sprout from my flesh."

"Whatever. Let's just get the teams picked," Wes mutters, shooting me an annoyed look.

He makes his first pick, and then Kyler goes, choosing me. I smile appreciatively at him then wait while Wes makes his choice. Kyler puts an arm around me and starts massaging my shoulder again. Although a few of his friends are staring at us curiously, Kyler doesn't seem to notice as he makes his next pick. Me, I notice. Like, way, way notice. Not just because he's touching me, but because he's touching me in front of his friends.

I probably hold my breath the entire time the teams are divided up. When there turns out to be an uneven number of players, Wes starts having a drama queen fit.

"I'll play." A girl with long brown hair pulled into a

side braid leaves the bleachers and crosses the field toward us. She looks about my age, but I don't recognize her from school. And unlike the other girls chilling on the sidelines, she's not decked out in heels and a dress, but a pair of skinny jeans and a plaid shirt over a black tank top.

"Lily, go sit your ass down," Wes barks at her. "You can't play football for shit."

She flips him the middle finger. "Neither can you."

Wes glowers at her. "Whatever. If you want to play, then play. But you're on Meyer's team."

"Good. That way, when we kick your ass, the win will feel that much sweeter." She grins haughtily at him then strolls up beside me. "Hey, only other girl crazy enough to play. I'm Lillian, but my friends call me Lily. And well, my dumbass brother, too." She throws a dirty look in Wes's direction.

"He's your brother?" I feel sorry for her. The guy kind of reminds me of a male version of Hannah. "He seems..."

"Like a jerk," she finishes for me. "Yeah, he is. But he's that way to everyone, so don't take it personally."

I wonder why but don't ask. "I'm Isabella, by the way. You can call me Isa."

"Isa. I like it." Her smile is so big it's nearly blinding. "I like your shoes, too. Totally killer."

I think she's just trying to be nice, but Lily's cheerfulness remains as we start the game. Either the girl was inhaling laughing gas before she came here, or she's one of the most genuinely happy people I've ever met.

For most of the game, Lily and I get put in positions that don't require a lot of moving or participating. While I wasn't too thrilled with playing, I do find it irking that the guys are taking over.

"Are you doing anything cool for Halloween?" Lily asks as we stand on the field, waiting for something eventful to happen.

"Honestly, I haven't really thought about it." Usually, I'm all about dressing up, but this year, I've been severely distracted by other stuff.

"You're dressing up, though, right?" She eyes me over from head to toe. "You look like the kind of person who dresses up."

"Is that a good thing?" I wonder, feeling insecure.

She nods, still all smiles and sunshine. "It's definitely a good thing. A lot of people think they're too old to dress up, but I plan on doing it for the rest of my life. It's too much fun to get all dolled up, you know. Why give it up just because society thinks you should stop having fun when you're a little bit older?"

"I completely agree. And, yes, I dress up, usually in something really over the top," I admit. "This year, I've been really busy, though, and haven't gotten around to deciding."

"You should go steampunk. You have a good look for it."

"You think so?"

"Oh, yeah. I can help you put something together if you want. I know where a lot of killer stores are, and I'm pretty awesome at sewing."

"Um… okay." I don't mean to sound hesitant, but considering how many times Hannah has set me up to think I'm making a friend, only to have it thrown in my face later, I can't help it.

For a tiny raindrop of a second, Lily's smile falters. "Or we don't have to. I just thought it might be cool to have a shopping buddy who enjoys Halloween as much as me. Most people can't handle how excited I get."

"No, it's cool. I want to go." I steal a glance at the bleachers. Most of the girls are watching the game, but two of Hannah's friends are staring at me while whispering to each other. I wonder if she's friends with them. Would it matter, though, if she's nice and everything?

"You don't like them, huh?" she says, not as a question but as a fact.

I fix my attention back on her and shrug. "It's more like they don't like me. Well, not all of them. But I don't know all of them."

She nods, as if completely understanding. "The two sitting on the top are pretty cool. They go to UW with Wes and Kyler. The three sitting toward the middle, I have no clue who they are, but they seem really into Kyler." I must pull a funny face or something, because she adds, "Don't worry, though. He seems into you."

I hate that I'm so transparent. "Do you know Kyler?"

She glances at the field where Kyler is dodging around guys with the ball cradled in his arms. "Since, like, I was four."

"Really? How?"

"He's been friends with Wes since then."

I don't recognize either one of them. "Do you guys go to Sunnyvale High?"

She snorts a laugh. "No. We're not that lucky."

Lucky? What? That makes no sense since Sunnyvale is a public school. "What do you mean?"

She pulls a *whoops* face. "It's nothing. I just meant that we weren't lucky enough to go to a high school that has such a great sports and art program."

Sunnyvale High may have a decent sports program, but their art program is nonexistent. The only art classes available are basic, beginner classes where you learn how to draw fruit in a bowl and generic nonsense like that. I don't call her out on her lie, though.

"So, do you go to UW, too?" I ask, even though she doesn't look old enough to be in college, but clearly, the high school topic is a touchy subject for her.

She shakes her head. "I'm actually supposed to be a senior this year, but I graduated early. I wanted to start classes at UW this year, but… My mom thought it would be a good idea for me to take a year off and save some money."

"Oh." Again, I can tell she's lying, but I don't want to press. "Where do you work?"

"I have two jobs, actually. One at the grocery store." She pulls a face. "And one at a second-hand store. That one's okay because a lot of old-school, cool stuff comes in, and the workers get first dibs. There was this really awesome old typewriter that I got and this 1940s cocktail dress that I bought for, like, ten bucks. I was going to wear it to prom, but…" She trails off, growing sober for a moment before she's bouncing off the walls. "You should come work there. The owner is hiring right now. It's a really fun, easy job, and it'd be nice to have someone cool to work with. Right now, the only person working there besides me is Mr. Belforid, who once showed up to work without pants on."

I choke on a laugh. "Really?"

She giggles. "Yeah, he's really old and got confused. He did have swim trunks on, thank God, but it was in the middle of winter, and he nearly froze to death."

After our laughter dies down, Lily turns serious again. "But seriously, you should come work there," she says. "I need someone sane to hang out with."

I hadn't thought too much about it, but since I'm going to be living with Grandma Stephy now, I should definitely consider getting a job so I can help out. "You know what? Maybe I will."

A smile expands across her face. I'm just starting to smile, too, when I hear my name being shouted.

"Isa, heads up!"

My gaze darts down the field in time to see Kyler throwing the football in my direction. I start to freak out as the ball soars through the sky and a herd of guys comes barreling at me. Sure, I know it's flag football, and they can't tackle me, but watching them run at full speed is super intimidating. At first, I contemplate just letting the ball hit the ground, but then I see Wes standing at the end of the field, looking bored, as if he's completely convinced I'm not going to catch it.

Screw this. I'm totally catching it and making a touchdown so I can do an awesome victory dance and throw it in his face.

Lily squeals and skitters out of the way as the guys charge toward me. Me, I run backward with my gaze locked on the ball and my hands in front of me. Wait for it. Wait for it. Wait… It lands right in my hands.

Hell yeah! I start to celebrate, but then Kyler yells, "Isa, run!" and I realize I still have to make it to the end zone. I reel around and run like a boss, trying to ignore the sounds of heavy footsteps charging toward me. Seconds later, I step over the line. Touchdown, baby!

I throw the ball down and do a dance until Kyler picks

me up and spins me around. I'm not even sure if we won, but it's all very exciting. It might have turned out to be a pretty good ending to a crappy starting day if at that very moment I didn't spot the dark blue car driving as slowly as possible on the road beside the field.

I try to convince myself it's not the same car, but then I see a Superman sticker on the back window. I'm pretty sure the car circling the park had the same sticker.

Kyler sets me down on the ground and raises his hand for a high-five. "See, pretty fun, right?"

I distractedly tap my palm against his. "Yeah, it kind of was."

"And the game's over, so you can celebrate that, too." He's beaming from ear to ear, his bare chest glistening with sweat.

I try not to gawk, but I steal a few glances at his ripped, defined muscles. "It's over?"

He laughs at me. "Yeah, you just scored the winning touchdown."

"Holy crap. I'm awesome," I joke, but my voice sounds flat. I can't seem to get into celebrating with that car right there.

"You are awesome." He drapes an arm around my shoulders. "And awesome people get rewards."

The scent of his cologne and sweat engulfs my nostrils. I'm not sure if I'm supposed to love the smell or hate it. Maybe a little of both.

"I get a reward?" I ask, and he nods. "What is it?"

He gives me a side hug and my heart flutters. "I'm taking you out for ice cream."

"Yeah!" I fist pump the air. "I'm so hungry."

"Just let me say goodbye to the guys and we'll go." He heads across the field toward his friends with his arm still slung around me, leaving me no other choice than to go with him.

I glance over my shoulder at the car and frown when I see it turning into the parking lot. I half-expect it to slam to a stop and a policeman to jump out of it. But all it does is stop by Kyler's car for a moment before flipping a bitch and speeding off.

I can't help thinking of the unknown texter for some reason and wondering if somehow the incidents are related. But how?

Maybe I'm just being paranoid, but I need to make sure to mention the car to Grandma Stephy just in case.

8

ISABELLA

WHILE SCORING THE TOUCHDOWN FELT EPIC, IT DIDN'T
earn me any mad cool points with Kyler's friends. I learn
quickly that I don't fit in with any of them besides Lily.
All the guys want to talk about is the big game next week
and whose party they're hitting up tonight. The girls talk
to each other until the party is mentioned, and then
they're all about the conversation, rattling off different
ideas. Once plans are finalized, they all part ways for
their cars.

Lily pulls me aside so we can exchange numbers, and
while I'm sending her a text so she has mine, I notice an
extraordinarily beautiful girl hugging Kyler.

"That's Jesmine. They dated before she dumped him
for some older dude," Lily explains when she notices me
staring at them.

"I don't remember them dating." I shove back the jealousy when Kyler doesn't seem in too big of a hurry to stop hugging Jesmine.

"It was over the summer and only lasted about a week." Lily slides her phone into her jacket pocket. "She's a couple of years older, too, so they spent a lot of time at college parties and stuff because she thought she was too cool for his friends. At least, that's what Wes says. I guess she got over it, though, since she's here. Or maybe it's okay now because most of his friends are in college."

I stab my nails into my palms, once again feeling like the dorky girl next-door harboring a silly crush on her sexy neighbor.

"Are you two, like, together, together?" Lily asks. "Because if you are, you might want to go break up the hug."

"Nah, we're just friends." Once I say it, I realize it's the truth. He can hug whomever he wants whenever he wants. It's not like we're a couple. Still, that doesn't mean I don't want to march over there and go all hungry zombie on both of them. Well, either that or go home and eat a gallon of ice cream.

Finally, the two of them pull away, but they don't put very much space between them. They lean in as they talk seriously about something, and he tucks a strand of hair behind her ear.

Ugh! I can't take this. It's like I'm back to square one, and if I'm being honest with myself, it's kind of a turn off.

"I have to make a call," I say to Lily.

She smiles at me, but there's a hint of pity in her eyes. "All right. Cool. Call me to get the details about the job, okay?"

I nod, wave to her, and then powerwalk to the car. I don't really have anyone to call, but I dial people's numbers, anyway, hoping someone will pick up. No one does, and I'm left with no other option than to climb into the car and pretend to mess around with my hair. Thankfully, Kyler climbs in only a couple of minutes later.

His cheeks are flushed. "Ready for that ice cream?"

I nod despite only wanting to go to my grandma Stephy's. "Sure."

He pauses as he's slipping the keys into the ignition. "Is something wrong?"

I shake my head, reaching over my shoulder for the seatbelt. "I'm just tired. Playing football is exhausting."

He doesn't appear like he's buying it. "She's just a friend."

"Huh?"

"Jesmine. I mean, we dated for, like, two seconds, but we both realized we weren't right for each other. Her dad passed away a couple of weeks ago, and I wasn't able to go to the funeral. This was the first time I've seen her since then."

"Oh. Okay." I'm so confused. Why is he telling me this? Because he can read the jealousy all over my face? Am I that transparent?

He puts a hand on my thigh. "I like you, Isa. Like, a lot. I'm sorry if I haven't made that clear."

"No… You have." God, I sound like a spaz. *Think of something else to say! Something awesomely epic!* "Um… I like you, too."

Not really awesomely epic, but it gets him to smile.

"Good. Now that we have that settled, let's get you some ice cream and then go back to the court." He shoves the car in park and backs out of the parking space. "I think there's still enough time for me to kick your butt one more time at horse."

I roll my eyes, but my joking attitude goes right out the window the moment we pull out onto the road, because that damn blue car pulls out right behind us.

9

KAI

THE DRIVE TO MAPLEVIEW IS LONG AND BORING. I'VE
never been one for driving solo, so I usually have a
driving buddy with me. I turn on some music to try to
liven things up, but when a Katy Perry song clicks on, all
I can think about is that time Isa and I danced to it, how I
licked her neck, pretending the move was playful when I
really just wanted to get a taste. She shocked the shit out
of me when she licked me back, but I think she did it
because she was drunk. Sober, I'm not so sure things
would've gone down that way.

Even if Isa liked me the way I like her, she's never
been the kind of girl to bluntly announce how she feels.
I've seen her dismiss a lot of things that probably
shouldn't have been dismissed. With a simple shrug or by

tucking her head down, she spends a lot of time pretending she's okay, even when she's not.

I've known this about her since we were in seventh grade. It was during the start of our brief friendship. Everyone in the entire school knew she was obsessed with Kyler, mainly because Hannah had blabbered it to anyone who would listen.

"Seriously, you should read her diary," I heard her saying to Kyler and a group of their friends during lunch. "It's all Kyler this, Kyler that. Kyler's so dreamy. I hope we get married some day. She even has some kind of weird chant thing written down on one of the pages that looks like a love spell or something. Seriously, she's such a stalker." Then she giggled in that shrill way that always made me want to jab my eardrums out. And, of course, her friends joined in like a bunch of wannabe hyenas.

Kyler didn't say anything at first, merely chewing on his burger. His friends all remained quiet, waiting for him to say something. And me ... While I sat at the same table, I never really joined in on their conversation. I was always just there, Kyler's younger brother, who everyone was nice to because my last name is Meyers.

"What do you mean there was a love spell?" Kyler finally asked, setting his burger down on the lunch tray in front of him. "Does she, like, think she's a witch or something?"

"Yeah, she talks about it all the time," Hannah said, but

I could tell she was lying, just like she was probably lying about the love spell and Isa having a diary at all—she didn't really seem like a diary kind of girl. "She thinks she can curse people and stuff." She wiggled her fingers in front of her, giggling. "You better watch out, Kyler. She might put a love spell on you, and the next thing you know, you'll be kissing her."

Kyler visibly shuddered, but I could tell it was more for show than over the fact that he was that creeped out about the idea of kissing Isa. I knew he hung out and played basketball with her sometimes, and there were a couple of times when I caught him staring at her balcony.

While Isa wasn't popular, she wasn't a hideous beast. She had clear skin; long, brown hair; and yeah, she was a bit on the gangly side, but her height made her awesome at shooting hoops. Her biggest problem was that she was super socially awkward and shy. Plus, she dressed really weird sometimes, wearing superhero shirts and even a cape once. And, yeah, while I thought superheroes and comics were cool, I knew better than to advertise it to the entire middle school. Although, I did envy her ability to be who she was, unlike me.

"There's no way in hell I'd ever kiss her." Kyler shot her a horrified look at the table where Isa was sitting by herself, eating lunch, and reading a book. "That'd be worse than kissing my dog."

"And you would know how?" I didn't even mean to say it aloud. It just sort of slipped out.

Kyler gave me his stupid I'm-the-shit-and-you're-not smirk. "You got a thing for weirdoes or something?"

"No." It was one word, but it felt like such a betrayal. I didn't defend her. I didn't do anything at all except sit there and listen to them as they started making fun of her. I was too afraid that, if I spoke up, they'd make fun of me. It made me no better than them, maybe even worse.

I hung out with Isa, and yeah, while I didn't declare to the world that she was my friend, I still sort of thought of her as one. She knew more about me than any of my other friends. She knew the real me. And she made me feel like I mattered, like I wasn't just Kyler's little brother who disappointed his father time and time again.

Things got progressively worse from there when Hannah stood up on her chair and announced to the entire cafeteria what she had just told Kyler. Almost everyone busted up laughing and stared at Isa.

I didn't laugh. All I did was watch as Isa quickly gathered her things and hurried out of the room with her head tucked down.

Later that day, when we were sitting in the hollowed out tree, I asked her if she was okay.

She simply shrugged, focusing on the drawing she was working on of a woman in a cape getup. "Yeah, I'm fine."

I stuffed a couple of chips in my mouth, trying to decide if she was really fine or not. She looked like she was unbothered, but how could she be? It would suck to get laughed at by everyone.

"Are you sure?" I slid closer to her. "Because you can tell me if you're not. I'm a great listener."

She paused, and I thought she was going to open up to me, but then she looked up and smiled. "What do you think of this drawing? Does it scream 'I'm a badass mofo about to save the world'? Or is it coming off too 'I'm a beotch'?"

It hurt that she didn't trust me, but then again, what had I done to earn her trust? Nothing at all. I was no better than everyone else.

"I like that she looks pretty badass," I said, hoping to at least get her to feel good about her drawing. "Who is she?"

Isa shrugged and used the pencil to shade in the woman's cape. "I'm not sure. I just see her in my head sometimes." She paused, pressing her lips together. "You really think she looks badass?"

I nodded. "Like she's about to save the world from every jerk out there."

She faintly smiled at that, like my words really meant something to her. It made me feel good about myself because the girl rarely smiled.

But that feeling quickly faded about a week later

when one of my so-called friends saw me hanging out with her. I had two choices in that moment: 1.) I could own it and finally just be who I was without hiding. But that would mean getting teased like crazy, and with everything going between my dad and me, I wasn't sure I could handle that. Or 2.) I could lie and cower out of the situation by calling her a stalker like Hannah did all the time.

I stupidly and very cowardly went with option two, and to this day, I still hate myself a little bit for it. Maybe I deserve to be in the position I am now—sitting here, trying to make money to pay a debt that isn't even mine while Isa is back in Sunnyvale with Kyler.

The thought, though probably true, is really effing depressing, so depressing I turn on my emo playlist simply so the music fits my mood.

Forty-five minutes and nine angsty songs later, I'm finally pulling into Mapleview. The town is a tiny blip on the map, even smaller than Sunnyvale, which says a lot.

After I circle the designated block three times without spotting a guy wearing a hoodie and brass knuckles, I grow worried he might be a no-show. Still, I drive around the block six more times before pulling over into the parking lot of a nearby gas station.

I'm not sure what to do. I don't have my phone, so I can't call Big Doug. He did say that, if I saw anyone sketchy, I wasn't supposed to drop off the envelope. But it's not like I've seen anyone sketchy; I just haven't seen anyone at all.

I make another few loops around the block, which basically consists of a few abandoned houses, a boarded up warehouse, and the gas station. Again, I don't see a single damn person, so I return to the gas station parking lot and sit in my car, trying to figure out what to do.

I pick up the envelope, turn it over, and fiddle with the clasp, debating whether to open it or not. I know Big Doug said not to, but dammit, I'm really curious what could be in this thing that's worth all this trouble.

I mess around with the clasp for a minute or two before setting the envelope back down without opening it. *If I want to get paid for this job, then I need to do it right.*

I climb out of my car and head for the gas station to see if the cashier will let me use their phone. But halfway across the parking lot, I realize that Big Doug is speed dial number seven in my phone, and I don't know his number.

"Shit. What the heck am I supposed to do now?" I curse under my breath, turning back around for the car.

That's when I spot a guy near my car, wearing a ski mask and holding a crowbar. When he raises the crowbar to break the window, I run at him.

"Don't you fucking dare!" I shout at him.

The guy is completely unfazed as he bashes the

crowbar against the window. The glass shatters, and he reaches inside, snatching up the envelope.

I barrel toward him, ready to beat his ass. But the closer I get, the more aware I become that the dude is fucking hella big, like sumo wrestler big. I slow down as I reach the back of my car, deliberating how far I want to take this. Sure, I promised Big Doug I'd guard the envelope with my life when I left, but I didn't mean that literally.

Sumo guy knows he can beat my ass, too, because he's just standing there, waiting for me to make a move.

I linger near the rear end of the car, keeping some space between us. "I'm going to call the cops on your ass if you don't give me that back." Sure, I don't have my phone on me, but he doesn't know that.

I swear I hear him laugh. Then he's suddenly striding toward me. Stepping back, I swing my fist around to punch him at the same time he raises the crowbar at me. My knuckles collide with his jaw as the metal bar slams against the side of my face. I hit the ground hard.

He hovers over me, grasping the crowbar. "Tell Big Doug his three strikes are up," he growls then raises the crowbar and whacks it against the side of my head.

Everything goes black.

10

ISABELLA

AFTER WE BUY OUR ICE CREAM, WE SIT IN THE CAR AND EAT it. I'm trying to be super cheery, but my thoughts are all over the place. I'm exhausted, on edge, and I'm sure I'm coming off as an energy draining downer. Despite the fact that the dark blue car hasn't made a grand appearance since we pulled into the ice cream shop, I can't shake the feeling it's going to materialize at any given moment. Even the cup of ice cream I'm holding doesn't help alleviate my worries.

"I still can't believe what you put in that." Kyler stares at the cup of ice cream in my hand, his face scrunched.

I can't help smiling as I replay the look he gave me when I ordered strawberry ice cream with cheesecake, sprinkles, cookies, gummy worms, and chocolate syrup toppings.

"You have no idea what you're missing out on. It's so yummy." I stuff a spoonful into my mouth to prove my point. "It took me years of trying out different concoctions to get it right, and all of the concoctions were good."

His lips quirk. "It took you that long to put together something that looks that disgusting?"

I stick my tongue out at him. "I've made ones that look way worse, like when I put gumballs and nuts into a cotton candy flavored ice cream. I almost threw that one up."

He makes another repulsed face. "That sounds so gross, but anything with cotton candy in it sounds gross to me."

My eyes widen. "You don't like cotton candy?"

He visibly shudders. "Ever since I was ten and ate an entire bag before I rode the Zipper at the carnival."

"Let me guess." I try not to laugh at how intensely serious he seems over the subject. "You threw up?"

"Yep. And trust me when I say it may taste good going down, but not so much when it comes up."

"I'll have to take your word for it, but I don't think it's going to stop me from eating cotton candy or cotton candy flavored ice cream."

"You're kind of crazy." A sudden, almost thoughtful expression appears on his face. "A crazy girl who makes touchdowns like a boss and likes the most disgusting looking ice cream I've ever seen."

"Hey, you can't mock the ice cream until you've tried it." I scoop up another spoonful, slowly put it into my mouth, and exaggerate a moan. "Mmm ... soooo good."

He stirs his cookie dough ice cream, his attention zeroed in on my mouth. "When you put it that way, it does kind of look tasty."

I feel my skin warm like gooey caramel. I try to think of something flirty to say, but my brain flatlines.

He stares at my mouth for a beat or two longer before dragging his gaze to meet mine. He pulls his bottom lip between his teeth. "Can I try it?"

"The ice cream?" My voice sounds unnaturally high.

He bites down harder on his lip, restraining a smile. "Sure."

For some reason, I don't think he meant the ice cream.

I take a subtle inhale, collecting myself before I speak again. "I don't know. It's not really for amateurs." I mentally high-five myself for how light and flirty my voice sounds.

He teasingly glares at me. "Come on, give me a taste. I can handle it."

I tap my finger against my lips, pretending to consider it. "Oh, fine. But if you hate it, don't blame me."

He grins, leans over the console, and opens his mouth.

My mouth goes dry. *Umm ... He wants me to feed him?* While Indigo taught me a thing or two about flirting, I was never able to do it as easily as she can. I always got nervous, and that was with guys we just met in clubs and stuff. This is Kyler—Kyler Meyers sitting here, waiting for me to feed him ice cream.

Willing my hand not to shake, I shovel up a spoonful of ice cream and move the spoon toward his mouth. His eyes are fixed on me as he waits. My heart is losing it inside my chest, throbbing like a song with a pulsating deep bass. My pulse only quickens when his lips wrap around the spoon, and he slowly sucks the ice cream off.

I've heard Indigo use the term erotic to refer to the sound of a guy's voice, the way someone dances, the way a guy she likes says her name. But I don't think I ever quite understood the term until now.

Kyler slants back, licking his lips, and his gaze floats upward as he lets the flavor sink into his taste buds.

"So, what do you think?" I must have a fairy godmother or something, because by some miracle, my voice comes out as smooth as taffy.

"It's not too bad." His lips spread into a grin as he steals a chunk of my ice cream with his spoon. "It's actually really good." He licks the ice cream off the spoon, and again, the word erotic flashes through my mind.

I'm not sure what my expression looks like, but something about it makes Kyler chuckle.

"I think, the next time we come back here, I just might get a cup for myself," he says, licking his spoon clean.

"Oh, yeah?" I ask. *Next time.* "Not brave enough to make up your own concoction?"

His lips part in mock shock. "Are you challenging me?"

"Maybe. I think the only way you could win the challenge is if you put some cotton candy flavored ice cream in it."

"Nope. Never gonna happen."

I shrug. "Then I guess you lose the challenge."

He considers something. "What would I get if I did it? What would you give me if, the next time we came here, I ate a whole bowl of cotton candy ice cream with any toppings you put on it."

"That challenge sounds dangerous. I get really excited about ice cream toppings."

"I didn't ask about the dangerous risks I'd be subjecting my taste buds to. What I asked is what I'd win if I did it. What would you give me?"

"Why would it have to be something I gave you?" I grin. "Wouldn't the reward be getting to eat awesome tasting ice cream?"

His eyes flare with something I can't quite decipher as his lips tug into a grin. "No, I'd definitely want something from you."

It's getting really, *really* hot in here.

I stuff another bite of ice cream into my mouth while I consider a reply. "Fine. What would you want?"

"I'm not sure yet. I definitely have to think about it for a while and make sure it's something really, *really* good."

"Well, when you decide, let me know."

"Oh, I definitely will." He winks at me before resting back in his seat.

I let a slow breath escape my lips. Mother of all hot chocolate syrup, that was one of the most intense flirting moments I've ever had.

Thankfully for my flushed skin's sake, Kyler changes the conversation to a much lighter topic before his phone buzzes. I think it's a text, but then he opens a calendar.

He sighs disappointedly. "And there goes our awesome moment."

"What is it?"

"A reminder that I need to write a paper for English."

"If you need to drop me off, that's cool," I say, not wanting to be a pain.

He waves me off, reclining back in the seat. "Nah. I can do it tomorrow." His head tips back as he gazes at the ceiling. "God, classes are killer. It makes me wish I appreciated high school more."

"What're you majoring in?" I pick a chunk of cheesecake out of my ice cream and pop it into my mouth.

"Right now, just general. I might change it eventually, but my dad ... He wants me to focus on sports right now." His jaw clenches, and I get the sense that maybe Kai isn't the only one who has issues with their dad.

"What about you? Do you want to focus on sports?"

"I guess so. I mean, I'm good at it, so I probably should."

"Being good at something doesn't mean you have to do it," I point out. "I'm good at basketball, but I never actually wanted to join a team. It was never my thing."

He turns his head to look at me. "What is your thing? I really want to know because it feels like I know you, yet I don't."

"My thing," I drum my finger against my lip, "is probably awesomeness," I joke then sigh. "I really don't know." I feel self-conscious to tell him about my manga obsession and how I love to draw my own comics.

"You like to draw, right?"

I nod. "It's not artsy stuff, though. It's more … comic stuff."

"That's cool." He cracks his knuckles. "Kai was into that stuff for a while. He had all these posters and stuff on his walls."

"Yeah, I know." I conceal a smile with a bite of ice cream. While I knew Kai was into comics, I never knew he had posters all over his walls.

A pucker forms at his brows. "How do you know? I don't think he ever told anyone, not even his friends."

"Back in seventh grade, we hung out for a while, and he told me then."

"You two hung out? I never saw you."

"It was after school."

He seems like he's tripping out over the idea. I don't know why. Is it that weird that Kai would hang out with me? Yeah, we were on two totally different social levels, but we have a lot in common.

"It's not that weird, is it?" I find myself asking.

Kyler straightens in the seat, shaking his head. "No, it's not that. It's just ... I don't know. It just surprises me. I mean, I know you guys hang out now, but I didn't realize you've been friends since then."

"We haven't been friends since then," I correct him. "We had a falling out that lasted pretty much until the beginning of this school year."

"What was the falling out over?" he wonders.

Um, yeah, there's no way I want to tell Kyler the story about how Kai called me a stalker when one of his friends caught us hanging out. It's too embarrassing, and with how much the two of them fight, I'm not sure how Kyler would react to the story.

"I don't know." I shrug. "Just middle school drama, and now we're over it."

He studies me intently, as if trying to unravel my thoughts. "But you two are just friends, right?"

For a microsecond, I'm thrown off by his question.

The slight pause lasts just long enough that the air between us shifts into awkward land.

"Yeah, we're just friends."

He assesses me for an uncomfortable amount of time before speaking again. "I still don't think you should hang out with him, not until he gets his shit together. You're too good for that."

"I'm not that good."

"Yeah, you are."

I want to argue, but he seems pretty adamant about it.

"So, you're into art and comics, huh?" He muses over the idea. "I've always wondered what you were drawing whenever I saw you sitting out on the balcony with your notebook."

I don't bother mentioning that I also spent time drawing him ... shirtless.

"I've been doing it since I was, like, six. It's really relaxing."

His lips pull into a lopsided grin. "You should show me some of your stuff sometime."

"Okay," I say, even though I'm uncertain he'd get my stuff.

"And teach me a thing or two about this whole comic world," he adds.

That gets me to smile. "I might consider it if you're lucky."

"Personally, I think I'm pretty lucky. I mean, I'm

sitting here with you, aren't I?" he asks with a charming grin.

I cover my mouth as laughter bubbles in my throat. He laughs, though, so I let it out.

He chuckles. "I know. I'm the worst. I don't know why I say shit like that. It just pops into my head."

"Maybe you should stop watching so many rom-coms," I tease, twisting the end of my ponytail around my finger.

He points a finger at me. "I never watch rom-coms."

"Yeah, right. I bet you do all the time," I tease. "I bet you watch them and memorize the lines."

He wiggles his fingers at me. "Don't make me tickle you again. Take it back or else."

I make a big show of zipping my lips together, and he dives for me, tickling me until I can barely breathe.

"Fine! I surrender," I gasp through my laughter. "You don't watch rom-coms."

He leans back, seeming satisfied. "Now say you'll show me your art."

I nod, catching my breath. "I'll show you whatever you want just as long as you stop tickling me."

He misses a beat, a strange look crossing his face. It takes me a second to process what I just said, but before I can get too mortified, he starts talking again.

"Okay, no more tickling," he says right as his phone vibrates again. He sighs, glancing at the screen. "And now it's reminding me to do my pre-Cal paper."

I draw a heart with an arrow going through it on the fogged up window. "Are you sure you don't need to take me home?"

"I said you were fine, and I meant it." He watches me add a thorny pattern around the heart like it's the most fascinating thing on the planet. "So, is that what you're going to college for? Art?"

My fingers fall from the window as a realization crashes down on me.

"I haven't thought much about it." Mostly because my family never really talked about it. College questions were always for Hannah. Me, I was just supposed to sit and listen. Listen and not be heard—those were the rules.

"I'm sure you'll figure it out," he says. "You still have time."

"Yeah, I know." On the inside, I'm freaking out. Art school sounds awesome, but isn't stuff like that expensive? Where would I get the money?

Suddenly, that job Lily suggested I apply for sounds like a good idea.

I remain stuck in my own head as Kyler starts the car and drives out onto the street.

"So, what's next on the distraction to-do list? We could go to the theater and watch a movie," he says as he cruises down Main Street. "One more game before we go hang out at your grandma's house? Whatever you want, name it, and it's done."

"Isn't it too dark to play basketball?" I stir the melted ice cream as I peer up at the dusty gray sky. A handful of stars are sprinkled across it, and the moon is shining brightly.

"Yeah, it might be." He flips on the brights. "I could always leave these bad boys on. I think the park has lights, too."

As awesome as Kyler has been, the events of today are gradually sinking in. I'm tired and worried, not just about what Lynn and my dad will do to me, but my future. I desperately need to talk to Indigo and Grandma Stephy, the two people who have pretty much been the only family I ever had. Besides, Kyler has other places to be. I heard him make plans to meet up with his friends at some party later tonight after hanging out with me.

"Kyler, I really appreciate everything you've done for me, but it's been such an intense day." I set down my empty cup of ice cream, crossing my fingers that I don't sound rude. "I kind of just want to go to my grandma's if that's okay."

He dims the car lights for a vehicle driving in the opposite direction. "Yeah, no. I totally understand. It's been a really hard day for you. You should probably relax." He pulls off to the side of the road and flips a U-turn, heading toward Sunnyvale Bay Community. "You want to stop somewhere and grab something to eat first? I was thinking maybe we could watch a movie or something when we get to your grandma's."

"What about that party your friends were talking about? I don't want to make you miss it. And you have those papers for school you need to work on. I feel like I'm stealing all your time."

"The party and homework can wait. I honestly don't feel like going out and partying tonight, anyway. I have to get up early for training and then spend the evening writing that paper."

"Are you sure you're okay with staying? Because I'll be fine at my grandma's if you want to just drop me off."

"Isa, I'm sure, so stop arguing." His voice is firm, but his eyes sparkle. "Besides, I was thinking maybe we could watch one of those zombie movies you love."

I perk up, lean back, and prop my feet up on the dash. "You like zombie movies?"

Shame crosses his face. "I actually haven't ever watched one."

"*Ever?*" What the hell of all apocalypses is happening right now?

He shrugs, looking like a kid who just got told he wasn't cool. "It's just never really been my thing. I'm more into sports movies and stuff. Is there, like, a sports zombie movie?"

"I don't think so. But I promise that, after tonight,

you'll no longer be a zombie movie virgin." Oh, my God, I can't believe I just said something unintentionally dirty like that. *Again.*

My cheeks flame like the goddamn sun. Fortunately, it's dark enough in the cab of the car, so I don't think he can see it. But I do notice his lips twitching, as if he's struggling not to laugh.

When he speaks, his voice sounds gruffer than normal. "That sounds really interesting."

I laugh to breeze over the situation, but I sound breathless. To stop myself from saying something else embarrassing, I focus on deciding what movie to ease him into his soon-to-be developing zombie obsession.

As I'm mentally going through my favorite list of zombie movies, his phone vibrates again. He collects it from out of the console, glances at the screen, and then grimaces before pressing talk.

"What's up?" he says into the phone. He momentarily remains quiet then says a lot of yeah and no several times and one maybe before glancing in my direction. "I'm actually kind of busy right now. Can it wait until a little bit later?" He frowns, seeming tense and kind of irritated. "Fine. I'll do it." He hangs up and tosses the phone into the console. "Isa, I hate to do this to you, but I need to bail out a little early. That was one of my friends on the phone. They did something pretty stupid and need my help fixing the mess."

"It's fine." I lower my feet to the floor and sit up. "I'm kind of tired, anyway. I'll probably end up falling asleep the second I sit down."

"Still, I feel like a jerk for leaving you alone ... I'll make this up to you. I promise." He pauses. "How about a zombie movie marathon and dinner next weekend?"

"You don't have to do that. I understand. Really—"

He places two fingers over my lips. "I know I don't have to, but I want to."

My breath falters as his touch sends the strangest tingling sensations throughout my body. His gaze briefly flicks to my lips then goes to the road again.

I will my voice to come out evenly. "How about we compromise? One zombie movie and one sports movie. That way, I don't scare you off. Zombie movie virgins need to be eased into the blood and gore."

He smiles, moving his fingers away from my mouth. He lets his fingertip trail downward to my chin, neck, and collarbone before returning his hand to the steering wheel. "Just as long as you let me pay for dinner."

My pulse throbs as I nod. "Sounds like you've got yourself a date." I instantly want to take back my bold comment, wondering if I'm being too forward. But Kyler smiles, seeming pretty content, so I decide to just own it.

We don't say much for the rest of the drive, and before I know it, we're turning into the apartment complex.

He's parking the car in front of my grandma Stephy's building when I receive a text message.

As I'm rummaging for my phone inside my jacket pocket, Kyler warily eyeballs the building in front of us. "I really hate the idea of leaving you here by yourself."

Most of the lights are off in all the apartments except for a few porch lights. It's only seven o'clock on a Saturday, but it's like everyone's in bed already. I'd chalk it up to old people time, but after meeting some of my grandma Stephy's crazy friends while we were in Europe, I wouldn't be surprised if some of them were out clubbing or something.

"I'll be fine. I promise. But I do have pretty good fighting skills, just in case." I make fists and laugh before swiping my finger across the screen of my phone.

"Mad fighting skills or not, I'd still feel a little bit better if I weren't leaving you here completely alone." He keeps his eyes fixed on the building, as if waiting for something terrible to do down.

Indigo: I got yours and Grandma Stephy's messages! I'm home right now! Where the heck r u?

"I actually won't be here alone. My cousin's here." I stuff the phone into my pocket and open the door. "Thanks for everything, Kyler. I had a lot of fun. If it weren't for you, I probably would've spent all day stressing out and eating my weight in cookies."

A soft laugh escapes his lips. "While I think you could

probably handle eating your weight in cookies and then some, I'm glad you had fun." He reaches forward, and his palm molds around my cheek. "And thanks for playing football with me. I know it bored you to death, but you actually kicked some ass at the end."

"It didn't bore me to death. It just ..." I trail off as he leans forward and places the gentlest kiss on the corner of my mouth, causing me to nearly choke on my nerves.

But I force myself to remain composed and focus on the kiss, the way he tastes, like cookie dough and strawberry ice cream, and his breath smells like gummy worms. So yummy.

My stomach briefly goes *kerplunk*, like I'm on a rollercoaster, but the feeling fades into a soft lull, leaving me wanting more.

"Sorry, I couldn't resist." He shifts back in his seat with a slightly confused yet somewhat pleased look on his face. "I'll call you tomorrow, okay?"

I nod then grab my bags and climb out of the car. He waits for me to get inside the apartment before he backs out of the parking space, which I greatly appreciate considering the whole thing with the blue car.

Through the window, I watch him drive away, only turning away when he disappears down the road.

"Holy crap, I can't believe that just happened," I say to myself, slumping against the wall. I try to sort my thoughts. While the kiss was amazing, it wasn't the firework show I'd been expecting. But then again, it only lasted maybe a half a second.

"What just happened?" Indigo asks as she walks out of the hallway, wearing a pair of plaid pajama bottom shorts and an oversized T-shirt, running a brush through her damp, auburn hair.

I let my arms go limp, my bags sliding off and dropping to the floor. "Kyler just kissed me. Well, kind of kissed me. It was on the corner of the mouth, so I'm not sure if it counts." I expect her to get all giddy, but she simply stands there, combing her hair. "That's a good thing," I feel the need to tell her. I flop down on the sofa, slip the elastic out of my hair, and run my fingers through my tangled hair, feeling as though I'm floating on clouds of marshmallows. "I've been dreaming of it happening forever."

"I know you have." She sets the brush down on the kitchen counter then sits down in the chair across from me, tucking her legs underneath her. "It's kind of bad timing, though."

"There's no such thing as bad timing when it comes to getting kissed by Kyler Meyers."

"Isa … You basically just got kicked out of your house, found out your mom is … Grandma Stephy told me what happened today. I hate to say it, because I'm all for kissing, but considering your emotional state, I don't think any guy should be kissing you right now."

"I'm not that emotionally unstable." When I say it, though, I feel a tremor inside me, bottled up pain trying to explode. I swallow it down, knowing once I let it out, it'll be yesterday all over again. "Really, I'm not."

She gives me a look. "No, you're just trying to live in the land of denial."

"I'm not living in the land of denial. If anything, I'm living in the land of who-the-hell-am-I?" I bite down on my lip until I taste blood. "Look, I'm just afraid that, once I let it all out, I won't be able to turn it off. Yesterday … When Lynn said my mom was dead … I nearly lost it." Hot tears pool in my eyes, and I attempt to blink them away. "If Kai didn't find me before I took off … I don't know what would've happened."

"Kai found you?" Her head angles to the side as her brows dip. "Where? When? And how the heck did you end up with Kyler, instead?"

Sighing, I sit up and give her a brief rundown of everything that happened over the last twenty-four hours, including the creepy car that kept showing up everywhere I went.

"You think it was your parents?" she asks after I finish. "Or Lynn and your dad, anyway … I'm sorry. I'm not sure what to call them anymore."

I pick at my nail polish. "Me, either."

She drums her fingers against her knee. "How about those douchey assholes we used to know?" The small smile that touches my lips encourages her to go on. "Or we could just refer to your dad as the sperm donor, 'cause that's kind of what he is. And Lynn can be the Botox bitch, and Hannah—"

"How about the half-sister from Hell."

"More like the she-devil from Hell. She doesn't even deserve the title of half-sister. She may be related to you by blood, but that bitch has never acted like an older sister. None of your family has ever really acted like your family."

"I know." But, God, do I wish I didn't know.

I coil a strand of my hair around my finger, thinking about Big Doug and how I haven't heard anything from him yet. "I wish I could find out more about my mom … even if she's …" I suck back the tears. "Even if she's dead like Lynn says, I still want to find out more about her. I mean, what about her parents? Maybe they're still alive. And what if she has kids? What if I have, like, a half-brother or sister somewhere I don't even know about? And what if they're, like, nice or something? What if there are people out there I can call family?" By the time I'm finished rambling, I'm out of breath, and Indigo's eyes are wide.

She blinks a few times, shaking her head. "Okay, first of all, you do have a family: me and Grandma Stephy. We're always here for you. You're not alone in any of this." I open my mouth to tell her I know that, but she talks over me. "And second, we're going to get to the bottom of this whole mystery of your mom. We just need to come up with a plan."

I pick at my thumbnail. "Actually, I have a guy looking into it already."

She looks taken aback. "Who?"

I shrug. "Just some guy Kai knows."

Suspicion fills her eyes. "And how does Kai know this guy?"

"It's just a friend of his."

"A friend who does what exactly?"

"I don't know. Looks stuff up on the computer, maybe. I'm not really sure. I didn't really ask too many questions when I met him." I scratch at my arms, squirming under her unwavering gaze. "Why are you acting so weird? It's not that big of a deal."

"Did you pay this guy?"

"No."

"So, let me get this straight. Kai introduced you to some random guy with a computer, who supposedly is going to look up stuff about your mom and do it all for free? Because let me tell you that sounds sketchy and like, eventually, you're going to have to pay for it."

"It's not sketchy," I argue, not bothering to mention I met Big Doug in a pool house with some really expen-sive-looking computer equipment and that I'm pretty sure he's a hacker. "He's Kai's friend. I'm sure that's why he's doing it for free."

"Hmmm." She doesn't seem too convinced. "I think I want to talk to Kai about this."

I'm about to tell her that's not necessary—after everything Kai's done for me, the last thing I want is for Indigo to give him the third degree—but then my phone goes crazy, an unknown number flashing across the screen, and I hesitate. I haven't heard anything from the unknown caller in the last two days. What if it's them? What if they've decided to start harassing me through calls now?

"Who is it?" Indigo wonders, braiding her hair.

My finger hovers over the talk button. "I don't recognize the number."

We sit there in silence as the phone rings three more times before it switches to voicemail.

I balance the phone on my knee. "I'm so afraid the cops are going to show up and drag me outta here. Every noise and out of place thing has me jumping out of my skin."

"Grandma Stephy took care of the whole police thing, and she wouldn't have told you she did unless she really has the situation handled."

"I know ... but I can't shake the feeling that Lynn has something else up her sleeve, and she's just waiting for the right moment."

Silence stretches between us as we both sit on my declaration. Then my stomach lets out a loud grumble, breaking the tension.

We both erupt in giggles.

"Have you eaten at all today?" she asks after our laughter dies down.

I drape my arm across my starving belly. "I had some ice cream. That's about it, though."

"I'll find us something to eat." Instead of heading for the kitchen, she walks over and gives me a hug. "I'm so sorry this is happening to you. And I'm so sorry I haven't really been there for you over the last couple of weeks. I've been a really shitty friend."

"You don't have to apologize." I hug her back. Sometimes, it still feels so strange getting hugs. Growing up in a household where no one really liked me, I rarely—if ever—got them. "You've been busy with work and stuff."

"I know, but still … I should've made time for us to hang out more, especially with everything you've been going through." She steps back. "You know what? Tomorrow, I'm going to blow off work, and you and I are going to drive into the city and go shopping."

"You don't have to do that. I promise I'm f—"

"Don't you dare say you're fine. You have a bad habit of doing that sometimes."

"Doing what?"

"Acting like you're fine even when you're not."

"I don't do that," I protest. "I mean, look at what I did yesterday. I totally lost it. Like, crying until I had no tears kind of lost it."

"Probably because you held it in all those years in that house," she says. "You dealt with all that shit and hardly ever complained about it once. If I were you, I would've lost it a long time ago."

"Maybe I did lose it a long time ago," I suggest. "Maybe that's why I'm so weird. Maybe my sanity button broke a long time ago."

"Maybe." She pats my head. "But we're still going shopping."

"Fine." I pick up my phone as it notifies me I have a voicemail. "Well, whoever it was left a message." I dial to my voicemail and chew on my thumbnail as I wait anxiously to see who called while Indigo wanders into the kitchen, eyeing me worriedly.

"*Hey, Isa, it's Kai ... I'm guessing you're either busy with Kyler still or not answering because some weird-ass number showed up on your screen, but I really need to talk to you.*" He pauses, and when he speaks again, tension pours from his voice. "*Okay ... I guess I'll call back in a few minutes. Hopefully, you'll answer.*"

When the message ends, I hang up. "That was Kai."

"What'd he want?" She grabs a box of macaroni and cheese from the cupboard and then closes the door.

"I don't know." I stare at my phone, willing him to call

back. "He sounded funny, like he was nervous or something."

My stomach winds into knots. What if this has something to do with T? What if he's in trouble somewhere? Or worse, what if he's hurt?

"Did he say he'd call back?" She flips over the box to read the instructions on the back.

"Yeah." I keep my eyes glued to the phone. *Come on, Kai. Just call back.*

A few minutes trickle by, and my phone remains silent. I'm just talking myself into dialing the number, seeing if Kai will answer, when my phone rings again. The unknown number crosses the screen, and I quickly answer it.

"Kai." For some reason, I sound like I just ran a marathon.

"Hey, you answered." A relieved exhale floats through the line. "I was worried maybe you didn't have your phone on you."

"Sorry I didn't answer the first time you called. I didn't recognize the number, and after the weird day I had …" No. Now's definitely not the time to get into that conversation with him. "Where are you? And whose phone are you calling from? Is everything all right? You sounded nervous on the message."

He chuckles, the sound like calming music to my ears. "Which one of those do you want me to answer first?"

"Umm ... How about, where are you?"

"In Mapleview."

"Still?"

He heaves a weighted sigh. "Look, it's a long story, but before I even attempt to get into it, I need to ask you for a favor."

"Whatever you need, I'm there." After how much Kai has done for me, I owe him about a gazillion favors.

It takes him a second to answer. "I need you to drive over to Big Doug's house and tell him something happened, that I'm stuck in Mapleview, and he needs to come pick me up. I'd call him, but I don't have my phone, and I can't remember his number."

"If you need a ride, I can come and pick you up," I find myself saying without even putting a lot of forethought into the decision.

"You mean you and Kyler can come pick me up, right? Because I don't want him knowing about this." A drop of jealousy lands in his tone, leaving me feeling guilty and sort of confused.

Is it because he despises Kyler that much, or is it something else? One thing I do know for certain is that the whole being friends with Kai while kind of dating Kyler thing is going to be pretty complicated since the two of them don't get along at all.

"I'm not with Kyler anymore," I tell Kai. "He dropped me off at my grandma Stephy's house a while ago. I'm with Indigo right now. And I'm sure she'll let me borrow the car."

"Oh, I will, will I?" Indigo says from over by the stove. She's only kidding, her expression laced with curiosity.

"It's okay," he says. "Big Doug can do it. I need to talk to him, anyway."

"Are you sure? Because I really don't mind." I don't, either. Yeah, I'm tired and in desperate need of a shower, but he sounds like he might be in trouble, and I want to help him like he's helped me. When he hesitates, I add, "If you don't let me, then I'm just going to sit around and worry all night. I probably won't get any sleep, and then I'll be cranky when Indigo takes me shopping tomorrow. She'll end up never taking me shopping again, and I'll be forced to wear the same clothes forever because I suck at shopping by myself, and honestly, being in a store alone kind of freaks me out."

"It does, does it?" He sounds amused.

"Um, yeah. It's like the worst place to be if an apocalypse happens," I continue on with my awesome story. "But, anyway, all my clothes will eventually get holes in them, and I'll end up having to go everywhere naked. I'll get kicked out of school because of their whole no being naked on school grounds policy, and I'll have no choice but to join a nunnery and wear their robes because it'll be the only way I'll ever be able to get clothes again."

His laughter fills the line. "A nun, huh? Because I can't picture you being a nun."

"Exactly. That's why you have to let me come and pick you up." I love that he sounds more relaxed and that I've played a part in it. It makes me feel like I did something right.

"Are you sure you don't mind?" He double-checks. "Because, honestly, I'd rather you come get me. I'm a little pissed at Big Doug right now."

I wonder why. I wonder what happened. I wonder a lot of things, but I can ask him all that when I pick him up.

"Yep. I'm already heading for the door," I say, dragging my ass off the couch. "Just tell me where you are."

He gives me the address, and I punch it into my notepad app. Then I tell him I'll be there in two hours tops, and he thanks me at least ten times.

After we hang up, I go into the kitchen to get the car keys from Indigo. "You're cool with me borrowing the car, right?"

She's turned off the stove and is dumping the water out of the pan and into the sink. "Grandma Stephy would chew my ass off if I let you drive by yourself to Mapleview this late."

"I doubt it. I mean, she's not strict. She let us run around all the time by ourselves on the trip." I zip my jacket up, cringing at the giant mud stain on it. I haven't changed or showered since yesterday morning. I can only imagine how I look and smell right now. "Besides, I'm almost eighteen."

"That doesn't matter." She puts the unopened box of macaroni and cheese into the cupboard. "You've had a rough day, and she won't want you being by yourself."

True. She told me that on the phone when I talked to her earlier.

"So, here's what we're going to do." She dries her hands on a dishrag. "I'm going to change into some clothes while you change yours, because that mud stain is going to drive me nuts. If I have to look at it the entire drive, I might just pull it off you and burn it." She smiles at me so I know she's kidding. Well, kind of kidding, at least about the burning part.

While she goes back to her room, I change into a pair of clean jeans, a long-sleeved black shirt, and slip on my favorite pair of red velvet boots. Then I hurry to the bathroom to wash my face, brush my teeth, and put on some deodorant. I don't bother looking in the mirror. I know it will only make me want to clean up more, and there's no time for that.

"Ready?" Indigo asks as she pokes her head into the bathroom.

Her hair is curled, and she's put on a touch of lip-gloss and mascara. She has on a skirt, knee highs, and a leather jacket, along with gladiator sandals. How the hell she managed to get all dressed up like that in five minutes is beyond me.

"You know we're just picking him up at some gas station, right?" I give a pressing glance to her outfit.

"Yeah, but I need to be prepared. You never know when you're going to run into the love of your life." She heads down the hallway. "For all I know, I could get a flat tire on the way there, and when I flag down someone for help, it could be the guy I'm supposed to fall in love with."

"Or the guy who's going to murder us and bury us in the woods," I say, following her. "Do you know how many scary movies start that way?"

She rolls her eyes as she collects her keys, purse, and phone from the kitchen counter. "Jesus, Isa. Why do you have to ruin my fun?"

"Just promise me you'll call a tow truck if we get a flat tire." I open the front door. "No flagging down cars ..." I suddenly get the feeling I'm being watched. My hair stands on end, and my heart rate accelerates as I get a bad case of the heebie-jeebies.

"What's wrong?" Indigo asks as she steps out onto the porch and locks the front door.

My gaze skims the parking lot, the buildings, the trees, the street. "It's nothing ... I just got the strangest feeling I was being watched."

She tosses the keys into her purse and zips it up.

"Okay, I think I'm banning you from scary movies for a while. It's not helping the situation."

I scratch at the back of my head, trying to figure out why I feel this way. No one's around. Even the parking lot is almost completely bare. "Sorry. I think I'm just really tired, and this blue car thing has me on edge."

"Totally understandable. And, like I said before, when Grandma Stephy gets home, we'll tell her about the car, but honestly, I wonder if it might've been either Hannah messing with you or maybe your dad or Lynn."

"Hannah doesn't have a blue car with a Superman sticker on it," I point out. And earlier when she denied sending the texts, I think she may have been telling the truth because she honestly seemed clueless about what was going on.

"So? She could've borrowed a car from one of her friends."

"Yeah, I guess so." Still, I can't see Hannah being friends with someone who would drive a car with a Superman sticker on it.

Indigo links arms with me and hauls me toward the car. "Come on. Let's go get your man candy."

I don't correct her about Kai being my man candy. I just follow her to the car and cross my fingers that we don't get a flat tire.

11

ISABELLA

By the time we make it to Mapleview, it's almost ten o'clock. Indigo tells me I should probably text Grandma Stephy so she doesn't freak out when she gets home and we aren't there. I send her a text, but she doesn't reply.

"She's probably still on the plane," Indigo says, ashing her cigarette out the window. "When was her flight supposed to land?"

"I'm not sure. She said she'd be home by eleven, though."

"I hope her flight doesn't get delayed. She'll come home all cranky if it does." She slows down the car as the speed limit drops. "What road was this gas station on?"

I open the notepad app and tell her the address. "I think it's on the east side of town."

She flicks her cigarette out the window and focuses

on the road. "This town is dead. Not a single store is open, and it's only ten o'clock on a Saturday night."

"Mapleview's like that," I tell her. "It's lower key than Sunnyvale."

She frowns at the stores bordering the street. All of them are closed up, the only lights coming from the lampposts. "It looks like a ghost town."

"It kind of is." I type the address into a map app so we can get directions. "I mean, people live here and everything, but it's the kind of place people live when they've done something shady or do stuff that's shady and don't want to be found."

"Then why's Kai here?"

"He probably was just visiting someone or something." But I know that's not true. He mentioned something about Big Doug getting him into this mess. I just wish I knew what kind of mess he was in. "Make a right off here." I point at a street sign.

Indigo does what I say and turns down the side road. The longer we drive, the sketchier the area gets: fewer lampposts line the streets; the stores turn into boarded up warehouses; and people have gathered in parking lots and street corners, doing God knows what. By the time I spot the gas station, I'm ready to grab Kai and say "peace out" to the town.

"There's his car." I point at it while unbuckling my seatbelt.

She pulls into the parking lot and parks next to Kai's car. That's when I notice the passenger side window is shattered, the hood is dented, and the headlights look cracked.

Indigo's eyes practically bulge out of her head as she takes in the condition of Kai's car. "Did he get in a wreck?"

"I have no idea." Panic sets in. What if he's hurt?

I jump out of the car and don't stop, even when Indigo shouts at me to wait a minute. By the time I fling the door open and stumble inside the gas station, I'm a nervous wreck, all wild-eyed and trying to catch my breath.

My gaze skims the gas station. I spot Kai sitting behind the counter at a table, playing poker with an older man who's wearing a button-down shirt with the gas station logo on it.

"I think you might be cheating," Kai says to the man, glancing down at the cards he's holding.

"Quit whining and make your bet," the old man grumbles, "before I make you wait outside."

Kai adds a few red poker chips to a small pile in the middle of the table. "Yeah, yeah, you've said that, like, twenty times."

"Well, this time, I mean it," he growls. "Whatcha got? I bet nothing."

"Ha!" Kai lays down his cards. "A full—" He catches sight of me. "Hey, you made it."

"Of course I made it." I smile back, but my smile falters when I see the bruises and cuts on his face. One of his eyes is so swollen I wonder if he can see out of it. A cut runs along his hairline, dry blood dots his cheek, and his lip is puffy. "Holy crap, Kai! What happened to your face?"

"What? It doesn't always look like that?" the old man asks, smirking at Kai. "Is this that girl you were yammering about being in love with?"

Ummm … What?

Kai seems unbothered by what the man said, grinning as he scoots the chair away from the table and stands up. "Quit trying to get me in trouble," he tells the man then turns to me. "I'll explain the face thing in the car."

"Okay." I keep my eyes on him as he rounds the counter, trying to tell if he's injured anywhere else.

Blood stains dot his long-sleeved gray shirt and jeans, and his face looks horrible, but other than that, I can't see anything else.

"Are you okay? Did you get hurt anywhere else?"

"You and your questions." He tsks at me, seeming in an oddly good mood considering how beaten up he looks. "You're always so full of them."

I cross my arms. "You call me from an unknown number, ask me to drive out to Mapleview to a random gas station in the middle of nowhere, and your car is all messed up, not to mention so is your face, so questions are totally justifiable right now."

Humor dances in his eyes. "Am I in trouble?"

I have to work really hard to appear angry. "Yes. At least until you start explaining."

He starts to suck his lip between his teeth, but there's a small gash on it, and he winces. "Are you going to punish me if I don't?"

I feel a flush heating my cheeks. "How can you joke right now when it looks like your face got into a fight with a rock and lost big time?"

"Actually, it was a sumo-sized dude and a crowbar." His shoulders sag. "Look, I know I messed up, but joking is the only thing keeping me from losing it."

His honesty throws me off. Usually, Kai jokes about everything and hardly ever admits his true feelings.

"Do we need to get anything before we go?" I glance around the store. "Maybe some band-aids and an icepack?"

He cups his cheek with his hand as if he's in pain. "An ice pack sounds nice."

"All right, let me grab some stuff, and I'll meet you in the car." I start for the back of the store.

He trails behind me down an aisle. "I just got my ass mugged right outside, and that was in broad daylight, so

I'm not about to let you wander around by yourself when it's dark."

I open the freezer door and grab a bottle of water. "Mugged by a sumo wrestler?"

"I know it sounds crazy, but it really happened." He dazes off, looking like he doesn't quite believe it himself. "I walked away from my car for, like, five seconds, and this guy shows up, breaks my window, steals ... something out of my car, then hits me over the head with a crowbar. I blacked out, and when I woke up, my car was all jacked up. He even destroyed the battery and slashed the tires. Stupid crazy bastard."

A few things run through my mind at once, but the biggest thing that stands out is, "He hit you over the head with a *crowbar*?" I reach for his head. "Do you have a concussion?"

"I'm not sure." He squints his eyes as my fingers brush across his hairline. "What does a concussion feel like?"

"I don't know. I've never had one before." Okay. Now I'm really starting to get worried. "I think we should take you to the hospital."

"No," he says firmly. "No hospitals. No doctors. My parents can't know about this."

"They're going to find out when you show up, looking like that." I gesture at his face.

He touches the corner of his eye and winces. "I know it's bad, but I can't tell them. They already ... my dad ...

I'm not going home. I'll just crash at Big Doug's house or something until my face heals." He doesn't seem too thrilled about that idea, though.

"That could take at least a week. Won't your mom and dad get mad when you don't come home for that long?" Isn't that what normal parents do?

"They won't care," he says. "They'll be glad I'm not there."

I remember the night I saw Kai's dad yell at him and smack him on the back of the head. While it wasn't very hard, it still didn't sit right with me. It makes me wonder if that's why he doesn't want to go home. Perhaps he's worried his dad will hit him or something. And then there's that thing Kyler said in the car about how his dad wants him to play sports. Clearly, their dad's a demanding guy, the complete opposite of my barely-there father.

I think about how scared I was to go home last night, how Kai stayed up and watched movies with me, and how we ended up falling asleep on the couch together when I thought I wasn't even going to be able to sleep at all.

"You can stay with me if you need to."

"At your grandma's house?"

"She won't care. She's nice. She'll probably make you sleep on the couch, but it's pretty comfortable. And she makes breakfast in the morning."

As he considers my offer, a series of emotions flash across his face: hesitancy, confusion, gratitude, and ultimately, hilarity. "Are you going to sleep on the couch with me?"

I roll my eyes. "No. You have to be a big boy and sleep all by yourself."

He juts out his lip, sulking. "But I slept on the couch with you. Doesn't that mean you have to return the favor?"

I smash my lips together to keep from smiling and encouraging him more. "I'll return the favor another time. My grandma's cool and everything, but not that cool."

Grinning, he reaches forward and traces his finger down the brim of my nose. "I'm going to make sure you follow through with that."

His touch makes me feel like I swallowed a jaw full of very alive, very excited butterflies. All from a freakin' touch.

Afraid my voice will come out all wobbly, I say nothing and search the store for an icepack. I end up settling on a cup full of ice, and then I grab a couple of napkins to clean up the blood with. The band-aids are a no-go, so I pick up a couple of candy bars and a soda, hoping a little sugar rush might help him feel better.

After we pay, he waves good-bye to the cashier, and then we head out to the car. Kai grabs a thin folder and his jacket out of his car before sliding into the backseat of my grandma Stephy's car.

Indigo rotates around in the seat, takes in the sight of his face, and her jaw drops. "Whoa. You look like shit."

"Gee, thanks," he says then sighs. "But seriously, thanks for coming to pick my sorry ass up. It was really cool of you."

"No worries." Indigo starts the engine. "You're okay, right?"

"I am now." He wiggles around, knocking his back against the seat. "I think this seat is busted." He reaches over and fiddles with a latch, folding the back of the seat forward and peering into the trunk. "Your grandma really needs to get this fixed."

"She won't," I say, sliding into the seat beside him. "She'll say it's old and has character and that fixing it would be ruining it."

Kai shoves the seat back, his eyes landing on me. "You don't have to sit back here with me. I promise I can handle sitting by myself for a couple of hours without getting into trouble."

"I don't know about that. You're kind of a handful." I set the bag of stuff I bought onto the floor and pull the door shut. "I'm going to try to clean up your face, okay?"

"Aw, my very own naughty nurse." He presses a hand against his chest. "I've always wanted one of those."

Indigo giggles as she drives out of the parking lot. "I forgot how adorable he is."

"Don't encourage him," I warn her. To Kai, I say, "I'm not your naughty nurse. I'm just trying to get you bandaged up, and then I'll try to see if I can find info about concussions."

He rubs his lips together, suppressing a smile. "Don't ruin my fun. Right now, I'm totally picturing you in a tight, short, white dress with knee-highs that go all the way up those long legs of yours." His gaze drags up my legs. "It looks really good on you, by the way."

Tingles spill across my skin, but I quickly shrug them off. I'm not sure whether to be happy he's in a good mood despite everything going on or worried that maybe it's a concussion making him act like this.

"Lean back in the seat," I instruct as I dig out the napkins and water. "I'm going to clean the blood off your face. Then you can press the cup of ice to your cheek while I do an internet search on concussions. Whatever you do, don't go to sleep, though. I think I remember reading something in health class about needing to stay awake after a concussion or something."

He pouts. "What if I'm tired, though?"

I wag a finger at him. "I don't care if you're tired. Keep your eyes open. If I even so much as see them starting to shut, I'll pinch you."

He lifts his hand to cover his mouth and hide a smile. "You're cute when you're bossy."

I suck a discreet inhale through my nose, trying to remain nonchalant. But I can't help thinking about Kyler and how, earlier today, he called my freckles cute. While I know Kai's just messing around with me, it still feels uncomfortable to have both of them call me cute on the same day.

After I settle my breathing down, I twist the lid off the bottle of water and pour a couple of drops onto a few napkins. "So, are you going to tell me what you were doing out in Mapleview?" I gently press the napkin to a dried spot of blood on his cheek.

He flinches but doesn't move his head, keeping his eyes trained on me. "I was doing something for Big Doug."

"What kind of something?" I delicately run the napkin against his cheek, slowly moving it toward his jawline.

"Just something."

"Something sketchy? Because Mapleview doesn't have the best rep for being a place where people go to do good things."

"Are you judging me?" He hugs the folder to his chest like a teddy bear, looking hurt.

"What? God, no... I'm just worried about you." I inch closer to him, press a couple of fingers to his other cheek, and tilt his head so I can clean off the blood on the other side of his face. "This morning, when we were in the hallway, you started to tell me something bad was going on with you and that T guy, but you never got a chance to finish."

"Because Kyler interrupted," he grumbles, scowling.

"I know. I wish he wouldn't have. I wanted to—I want to make sure you're okay."

"I'm okay." His gaze is so intense, so fixed solely on me, that my fingers tremble. "You guys hung out all day?"

I reluctantly nod. "Well, until about seven."

"What did you guys do?" he asks, not really sounding like he's sure he wants to know.

I shrug, turning on the ceiling light to get a better look at the cut on his forehead. "Played basketball for a little bit. Then we went to the football field and played flag football with his friends."

"Ew," Indigo says, and I realize she's been listening to our entire conversation. "Football? That's what you guys did all day?"

It makes me a tiny bit uneasy that she's paying so much attention to Kai and me. Indigo is too observant for her own good, and she's got a soft spot for Kai. She's determined Kai and I belong together, despite never having met Kyler, and is very blunt about her opinion.

"It wasn't that bad. I even scored the winning touch-down." I examine Kai's face to make sure I got all the blood off.

As I'm leaning over him, he starts combing his fingers through my hair. The movement, while subtle, centers all of my attention there. I become hyperaware that his face is two inches from my neck, the warmth of his breath tickling my skin.

"Touchdown or not, it still had to suck balls playing with his friends. They're such dicks, and I know they've been mean to you in the past." He makes a face. "I bet they were super nice to you now, though, just like Kyler, because you're hot. They don't even know you, not like I know you," he murmurs, fixated on playing with my hair. "Your hair's so soft. It reminds me of velvet."

I sit back to get a good look at him. "I think I need to look up symptoms of a concussion."

"I'm fine," he insists, resting his head back against the seat and lowering his eyelids. "Totally ... fine ..."

Panicking, I pinch his arm.

His eyelids pop open, and he glares at me. "Ow. That hurt."

"I warned you I'd do it." I take out my phone. "Now keep your eyes open while I look this up."

"Yes, boss," he mumbles, resting his head on my shoulder.

Indigo catches my eye in the rearview mirror, and even though I can't see her mouth, I know she's smiling. Me, not so much. I'm starting to get worried. Kai's acting like he's drunk or something. Maybe he is. But he doesn't have alcohol breath or anything.

It takes me fifteen minutes of fighting with an in and out signal before I can pull up a useful web page. I have to pinch Kai three times to keep him awake, and each time he responds, he makes less sense. Confusion is a symptom, and he's definitely confused. When I ask him questions about the last couple of hours, he can't even remember how he started playing poker with the cashier at the gas station.

"What about right after you were hit by that guy?" I ask him. "Can you remember what happened then?"

"Yeah, I blacked out for a minute, woke up, called you because I have your number memorized." He presses two fingers to his temple. "It's all up here. Every single number engrained into my mind … And I knew, if I called you, you'd help me without judging me." He strokes my cheek with his fingers. "You're so nice like that. Too nice, honestly. Too nice to be with me or my brother or anyone. No one's worthy."

At this point, his touches and rambling don't faze me. He clearly has a head injury, and while he doesn't want to go to the hospital, I'm not sure I feel okay with not taking him. Not knowing what else to do, I call Grandma Stephy.

"Where are you?" she asks the moment she picks up.

"Didn't you get my message?" I ask. "I left you one."

"Yeah, but it doesn't mean I'm just going to be okay coming home to an empty house after everything that happened today." She sounds mad. "And I tried to call you a ton of times, but your phone kept going to voicemail."

"Sorry." I feel bad for making her worry. "We were in Mapleview, picking up one of my friends who needed a ride. It was kind of a last minute thing. His car ... broke down, and he was stuck there."

"Are you heading home now?" she asks, calming down.

"Yeah, we're about fifteen minutes ..." I stammer over my words as Kai lies down and puts his head in my lap. "Um, yeah, we're about fifteen minutes out."

"Good," she says. "I don't like you being out this late, especially with everything going on."

I think about all the crazy stuff she let Indigo and me do while we were overseas. It doesn't make sense that she'd be worried about us being out late now. Then again, a lot has happened in the last couple of weeks.

I give Kai's arm a soft pinch since he starts to drift to sleep again.

"Grandma, do you know anything about concussions?"

"Why?" she asks warily.

I explain to her how Kai was mugged and hit over the head with a crowbar, and now he refuses to go to the hospital because he's worried his parents will get mad at him. When she questions why he's so worried his parents will get angry with him, I don't know what to tell her.

"Was he not supposed to be in Mapleview?" she asks. "Did his parents not know he was out there?"

"I don't know." I look down at Kai lying on his side, his face nuzzled in my lap. I have the craziest urge to run my fingers through his hair, do the same thing he did to me just minutes ago. I restrain the urge, though, telling myself I don't have a concussion, so I don't have an excuse to touch him like that. "I think he just doesn't get along very well with his parents. I think he's just worried his dad will get mad at him for the car getting ruined and stuff."

"His dad sounds like an asshole," she says matter-of-factly. "If he got mugged, then it wasn't his fault."

"His dad is kind of an asshole. He kind of reminds me of Lynn, only not so out to get you. He's just kind of a mean, angry guy." Poor Kai. I absentmindedly slip a few fingers through his hair but then quickly pull away. Whoa. What am I doing?

"Don't stop," he mumbles, reaching for my hand and moving it back to his head. "That feels so good."

I stare down at my hand with uncertainty. Should I do it? Isn't it weird?

"Just do it," Indigo urges. "He probably won't remember it in the morning, so you won't have to worry about things being awkward, but he'll be grateful for it tonight."

Maybe not awkward for him, but I just spent the day with his brother and let him kiss me on the corner of my mouth. And now what? I'm going to sit back here with Kai and play with his hair? Isn't that crossing a line? But since he's hurt, I somehow rationalize that it's okay and lightly run my fingers through his hair.

It's so soft...

"Isa, what's going on?" Grandma Stephy says through the phone, startling me.

I completely forgot I was talking to her.

"Nothing." No, it's definitely something. "What should I do about the concussion? Do you think he'll be okay if I don't take him to a doctor?"

"I'm not sure. I don't know much about concussions." She pauses. "I have a friend who's a retired doctor. He lives a few buildings down. Let me give him a call to see if he's still awake. Maybe he can help us out."

I recline back in the seat with my fingers still in Kai's hair. "Thanks, Grandma."

"You can thank me by getting your ass home. I'll feel better when you're here."

Yeah, me, too, but mostly because I just want to make sure Kai's okay.

By the time I hang up, we're almost to the apartment complex. Kai still has his head on my lap when we turn into the parking lot, and I'm still combing my fingers through his hair. I don't know why, but I'm starting to find the movement almost as soothing as he does.

"Kai," I whisper as Indigo shuts off the engine. "We're here." When he doesn't respond, I talk more loudly, leaning closer. "Kai, we're at my grandma's house. You have to get up so we can go inside."

The only answer I get is the soft sound of his breathing.

"Kai." I pinch him. Nothing. Panic. Panic. Panic. "Kai, you have to wake up."

"I am awake," he groans. "So quit yelling."

Relief washes over me at the sound of his voice. "Come on. I'll help you walk in, but I can't carry you."

He rolls to his back, and his eyelids flutter as he opens his eyes. He blinks up at me, dazed and confused. "Where are we?"

"At my grandma's," I tell him. "Remember, I said you could stay here."

He doesn't seem to have a clue what I'm talking about but sits up, anyway. He remains quiet as he opens the door and stumbles outside into the cool night air. I hurry and hop out, chasing after him as he wanders across the grass, heading in the wrong direction.

"Nope, this way." I catch his arm and haul him in the opposite direction.

He follows me, blinking around at the surroundings,

being strangely quiet for Kai. I don't relax when I get him inside. If anything, I freak out even more. In the light, he looks so much worse. His eyes are bloodshot, his expression dazed. Thankfully, my grandma's doctor friend is already there.

He's an older guy, probably in his seventies, with salt and pepper hair. He seems nice enough as he tells Kai to sit down on the sofa then pulls a chair up and asks him a series of questions. Kai answers the best he can. Then the doctor checks his reflexes. I decide to mention to the doctor that I think Kai also hurt his ribs so he'll check them out, too. I don't bother mentioning that it was from yesterday, because I don't even want to attempt explaining why Kai's getting beaten up so much. I couldn't even if I tried since Kai hasn't explained what happened yet.

"I'm sure he's fine," Indigo tries to reassure me.

"Yeah, I know." But I don't know for sure. I don't know much of anything anymore. I'm becoming the most clueless girl in the world. Isabella Anders, the clueless girl who doesn't know who her mother is, who plays with a guys' hair after she kind of, sort of kissed another guy, who's so worried sick right now she feels like she's going to puke.

Indigo offers me some cookies. "You need to eat."

I grab a handful and stuff them into my mouth, but I barely taste them. "I'll feel better when I know he's okay."

"I wonder why that is." Her accusing gaze bores a hole into the side of my head, but I refuse to look at her.

After the doctor finishes, he gets up from the chair and addresses Grandma Stephy. "He has a mild concussion, and that cut on his head might need a couple of stitches." He looks at me. "I tried to tell him he might need to get it taken care of, but he says he's fine. I don't have anything to stitch him up here, so I suggest trying to get him to go in the morning. As for the ribs, he may have broken one, but there's not much I can do for that. He'll just need to take it easy. He could go in and get an x-ray to confirm it, but that's about it."

I nod, but considering how adamant Kai was about not going to the hospital, I don't think I will be able to persuade him.

The doctor makes a list of symptoms to watch out for and says that, if he shows any signs of them, take him to the hospital right away. Then he gathers his stuff, and Grandma Stephy walks him out.

Kai's gaze collides with mine from across the room, and he pats the cushion beside him. "Come and sit with me and play with my hair some more." He seems more alert than he did in the car, but the wounds on his face are more prominent under the light.

When I dither, Indigo nudges me in the back with her elbow, shoving me forward. "Go and take care of your man candy."

I shoot her a dirty look, but she only laughs at me.

Shaking my head, I pad across the room and sit down on the chair beside Kai. "Do you need anything? The doctor said you could take a couple of painkillers, and I think my grandma might have an ice pack in the freezer."

He lies down and puts his head on my lap again. "I just want to rest like this."

"Is my lap that comfortable?" I joke, smiling down at him.

He bobs his head up and down, looking up at me, all serious and intense like he gets sometimes. "It's better than a pillow."

"I highly doubt that."

"Ha. Then you clearly haven't rested in your lap before."

"That's kind of impossible."

"Maybe." He drapes his arm across his forehead, shielding his eyes from the light as he stares up at me. "You should try my lap, then. It might be as comfortable."

"How would we ever know for sure, though? It's not like we can compare."

"True. But I think we should at least try." He starts to sit up; I guess so I can lie on his lap.

I place my hand on his chest and guide him back down. "We can try that tomorrow. Tonight, you rest."

"You promise?"

"Promise what?"

"That you'll put your head in my lap tomorrow."

I think about how Indigo and the doctor said Kai might not remember much about tonight. "Sure."

He smiles up at me. "You're so pretty, like seriously gorgeous. I've thought that for a while."

Indigo chokes on a laugh, spitting pieces of cookie all over the carpet. "He's even charming when he's completely out of it."

He's more charming if you ask me, but even though he's kind of a flirt normally, he's never flat-out told me I'm gorgeous.

Unsure what else to say, I trace a line with my fingertip around the cut on his forehead. "You should listen to the doctor and go to get stitches. He said you could end up with a noticeable scar if you don't, and it'll take more time to heal."

He waves me off. "Scars are cool."

"Not on your face."

"Uh-huh. It shows you're tough, that you've done crazy stuff. And it helps you remember when you did that crazy stuff."

"Do you really want to remember the crazy stuff that happened tonight?"

His expression sinks. "Isa, I think I messed up." He reaches up, circles his fingers around my wrist, and lifts my hand away from his face. At first, I think it's because I'm hurting him, but then he positions it on his scruffy, swollen cheek and sighs. "With this T guy … with what happened tonight … with the stuff I haven't told you yet …"

My forehead furrows. "What stuff haven't you told me?"

His lips part, his eyes flooding with worry, but before he can say anything, my grandma walks in. She takes one look at me and Kai on the sofa then shakes her head.

"All right, the boy sleeps on the couch," she announces, pointing at the hallway. "Isa, you're sleeping in the back guest room. You can set an alarm to come and check on him in a couple of hours." She grabs the handle of a suitcase propped against a wall near the door. "I'm going to go and take a shower. Isa, before you get into bed, you and I need to talk." With that, she walks out of the room, dragging her suitcase with her. Indigo starts to open her mouth, but before she can say anything, Grandma calls out, "Indigo, give Isa a moment to kiss her cute boyfriend goodnight."

Indigo chokes on another mouthful of cookie while mortification sweeps across my face. Oh, my God, did she seriously just say that?

My embarrassment only amplifies when Kai chuckles. "She thinks we're dating," he singsongs with his eyes closed, sounding completely entertained by the idea. "And that I'm cute."

"She thinks everyone's cute," I tell him, wanting to crawl into a hole and die.

His eyelids slowly open, and he squints against the light as he focuses on my face. "Yeah, but does she think every guy's your boyfriend?"

I almost say, "Yeah, she does. She's said similar things about Kyler." Thank God I manage to stop myself; otherwise, I would've made the situation even more awkward.

"You should let me up so you can get some rest," I tell Kai. "I'll come and check on you in a bit."

He grunts a protest but sits up and lets me off the sofa. I go to the linen closet and get him a blanket and a pillow. By the time I return, he's fast asleep on his side. I slip the pillow under his head and then cover him with a blanket before heading for the hallway.

Indigo is in the kitchen, getting a soda from the fridge. She looks up at me as I pass by. "That was sweet of you. It kind of seems like something a girlfriend would do for her boyfriend."

I scowl at her then smile so she knows I'm not really mad. "I'm not going to just leave him there without a blanket. Grandma lets her house get super cold at night."

"That's because she has hot flashes." She pops the tab on the can of soda. "It gets really bad when Harry sleeps over. The two of them go at it like rabbits all night and then crank down the heater when they're done because they get too hot."

I cover my ears with my hands. "TMI."

She laughs, takes a sip of her soda, and then motions for me to follow her as she heads for her bedroom. "We better get to sleep. We're still going shopping tomorrow, even if you gripe that you're too tired."

"Maybe we should go next weekend when stuff's calmed down."

"Nope. I've got my heart set on a new pair of shoes, and my heart always gets what it wants." She slips an elastic off her wrist and twists her hair up in a messy bun. "Besides, the last thing you need to do is sit around in this house, thinking about stuff. You need to get out and get some fresh air—breathe some Sunnyvale-free air."

"Fine, I'll go." I sigh. "But Kai's probably going to have to go with us since I told him he could stay here for a while."

"I'm completely fine with that. He seems nice and fun. Honestly, if he weren't so in love with you, I'd probably try to date him."

I feel the slightest pang of jealousy at the idea of Indigo and Kai dating. "He's not in love with me." Although, according to the cranky, old man at the gas station, he is. But Kai probably had a concussion the whole time he talked to him and probably wasn't making a lot of sense.

"Are you being serious right now?" She stops in front of her bedroom door. "Because, if you are, then I've clearly taught you nothing." She points a finger toward the end of the hallway. "Take it from me; that boy's in love with you. All that stuff he said in the car ..." She gets this swoony, goofy smile on her face. "Oh, my God, what I'd give for a guy to say something like that to me."

"He has a concussion. He didn't even know what he was saying."

"He might not remember what he said, but everything he did say tells me he's thought about you before: about knowing your number, about no one being good enough for you, about how gorgeous and amazing you are."

I squirm self-consciously. "I really don't think you're right." But deep down, a tiny part of me wishes she is. I don't know what to do with the feeling or if I should do anything with the feeling at all.

"Of course you don't, because your stupid fucking family stripped every ounce of confidence away from you." Her expression softens. "Sorry. I didn't mean for that to come out so rude."

"You weren't being rude. They've messed me up. I know that." I swallow the lump in my throat and turn toward the guest bedroom across from Indigo's. "I should probably get ready for bed then go and talk to Grandma, or else I'm going to get no sleep."

She sighs but lets me leave. When I get into the room, I close the door and recline against it. All I want to do is lie down in the bed and go to sleep, forget this day and yesterday ever happened. But I have a feeling these last twenty-four hours of revelations and stress are just the beginning.

After I pull on a tank top and a pair of red plaid pajama bottoms, I pad down the hallway and rap on Grandma Stephy's door.

"What're you knocking for?" she calls out. "Open the door and get your butt in here."

I twist the doorknob and enter. She's sitting on the foot of her bed, dressed in a matching shirt and bottom pajama set. A lamp is on and the door to the attached bathroom is open, allowing lingering steam to dampen the air.

"What did you want to talk to me about?" I ask. "Is it about Kai sleeping here? Because I didn't think it'd be that big of a deal."

She waves me off, patting the spot beside her. "I don't care about that. Although, I am curious how you ended up with him when you told me you were with Kyler this afternoon."

"It's a long story," I say through a yawn. "I'm glad you're cool with Kai staying here, though, because I kind of told him he could crash on the sofa for a week."

"Am I running a motel now?"

"I'm sorry. I know it's a lot—taking me in and letting Indigo live here—but he doesn't want to go home until his face heals, and I didn't want him to be homeless."

"He has nowhere else he can stay?"

I shrug, not wanting to lie to her but not wanting to tell her yes, either. For some reason, and I can't really explain why, I don't like the idea of Kai crashing at Big Doug's place. Maybe it's because whatever he was in Mapleview for had something to do with Big Doug. Or maybe it's because I'm not even sure where Big Doug lives. The only time I ever met him was in that rundown pool house, and the thought of Kai sleeping there wigs me out.

"I don't care if he stays here, just as long as he sleeps on the couch and you sleep in the bedroom." She gives me a stern look.

Just what does she think is going to happen?

"You know he's just a friend, right?"

"Friend or not, I still don't want you two canoodling. He looks like the kind of guy who would do that."

"He's not as bad as he looks. He's just had a rough night. We all have those. I had one last night, and he was there for me."

She puts her interrogation face on, crossing her arms and staring me down. "What do you mean he was there for you? Did you sleep at his house last night?"

"No." The lie shows through my voice. "Okay, fine. I did, but nothing happened. We just watched movies until we fell asleep. It's not like I could go home."

"You could've called Indigo to come and get you," she says. "You can always call us, Isa, no matter what."

"I know that, but ..." I shrug, unsure what else to say. "Kai helped calm me down, and I don't know ... I didn't really think much about calling anyone else."

"Hmmm..." She presses her lips together, studying me closely.

Her scrutiny makes me all squirrely. What the hell is she looking for?

"Well, I'm glad you had someone there for you," she finally says. "But from now on, no more spending the night with boys, got it?"

I salute her. "Yes, ma'am. And thanks for letting me stay here. And Kai. And for calling your doctor friend and my parents. Really, just thanks for everything. I promise I'm going to make this up to you."

"Don't worry about that." She draws me in for a hug. "Right now, all I want you to do is worry about graduating high school and deciding which boy you want to date. I know it seems fun to date more than one, but trust me when I say it can get pretty complicated."

Great. Now she's got it in her head that I'm dating Kyler and Kai. I could argue with her, but I don't see the point. She'll just keep saying the same things until I agree with her, and I have bigger problems to worry about.

"About my dad." I lean back to look at her. "On the

phone, you said his company was in trouble. What'd you mean by that?"

"I don't know the whole story, but I know they've been doing some iffy stuff, and now the company is under investigation. I threw it in his face on the phone because I knew it'd scare him enough to back off. The last thing he needs is for the police to dig around in his personal life on top of his business." She smoothes her hand over my head. "I don't want you worrying about that stuff. Like I said, I just want you to focus on being a teenager."

"What about my mom? Lynn said she was dead, but I still want to find out more about her."

"We will. I have a friend who's a retired cop. He might know where we can start."

"Man, you have all sorts of awesome friends, don't you?"

"I'm telling you. These retirement communities are where all the cool kids go."

We trade a smile and a hug, and then she shoos me out of the room, telling me to get my butt to bed. But I pause in the doorway and quickly tell her about the car I saw everywhere.

"What do you think about it?" I ask when I've finished telling her.

Her forehead creases as she shakes her head. "I'm really not sure, hon. It might just be Hannah trying to mess with you like Indigo said, but I think we should keep our eyes open and be extra careful, especially with those texts you've been getting. Don't go wandering off anywhere alone. If you do see it again, try to get the plate number."

"Why? Are you going to have your cop friend run the plates?" I'm partially joking, so it surprises me when she nods.

"Yep. I sure as hell am," she says. "If someone's harassing you, I'll track the bastard or bitch down."

I smile at that. "Love you, Grandma."

She fluffs a pillow, getting ready to climb into bed. "Love you, too, sweetie. I'm really glad you're here."

Her words warm my soul.

I head out of her room, feeling better than I did earlier today. Before I go to the guestroom, I check on Kai. He's fast asleep with the blanket kicked off, murmuring something about ninja kicking someone's ass. I giggle under my breath at how cute he looks then head to the guestroom and climb into bed.

As I lie there, trying to fall asleep, I tell myself everything will be okay, that I just need to do what my grandma says and focus on being a teenager. But in reality, I know there's no way I can do that, not with everything going on.

I'm afraid I won't ever find out who my mom really was. I'm afraid I will find out Lynn was right, that she was a terrible person who did terrible things and gave me up to my dad because she didn't want me anymore. I realize right then and there what might just be one of my greatest fears.

That my mother might have never wanted me.

ABOUT THE AUTHOR

Jessica Sorensen is a *New York Times* and *USA Today* best-selling author who lives in the snowy mountains of Wyoming. When she's not writing, she spends her time reading and hanging out with her family.

ALSO BY JESSICA SORENSEN

The Sunnyvale Mysteries:

Isa & the Guy Next Door

Isa & the Mystery

Isa & the Deal

The Year of Love & Whispered Truth

The Year of Promises & First Kiss

Untitled (coming soon)

The Unexpected Series:

Ensley & the Popular Guy

Untitled (coming soon)

The Honeyton Mysteries:

Hadley & the Guy Next Door

The Deal & a Secret

The Mystery & a Kiss

Untitled (coming soon)

The Alexis Files:

Sweet Little Lies

Truths & a Mystery

Secrets & the Spies

Confessions & a Secret (coming soon)

My Life with the Band

Discovering Benton

Whispered Secrets & a Kiss

Untitled (coming soon)

The Illusion Series:

The Illusion of Annabella

The Mysteries of Star Grove

Suspicion

Untitled (coming soon)

Rules of Willow & Beck:

Rules of Willow & Beck

Untitled (coming soon)

The Confession of Luna:

The Confessions of Luna

Untitled (coming soon)

Secrets Never Die:

Secrets Never Die

Untitled (coming soon)

Lexi Ashford Series:

The Diary of Lexi Ashford

The Diary of Lexi Ashford: The Agreement

Untitled (coming soon)

The Heartbreaker Society:

The Opposite of Ordinary

The Simplicity in Ordinary

Untitled (coming soon)

The Unraveling Mysteries Series:

The Mysterious Guy Next Door

The Mystery of the Symbol

The Forgotten Memory

The Suspicious Note

Untitled (coming soon)

A Pact Between the Forgotten:

The Art of Being Friends

The Rules of Being Friends

The Art of Kissing (coming soon)

Shadow Cove Series:

Spies & Sprinkles

Secrets & Vanilla Bean Frosting (coming soon)

The Coincidence Series:

The Coincidence of Callie and Kayden

The Redemption of Callie and Kayden

The Destiny of Violet and Luke

The Truth of Violet and Luke

The Promise of Violet and Luke

The Evermore of Callie and Kayden

Seth & Greyson

The Coincidence Mysteries:

Callie & the Start of a Mystery

Untitled (coming soon)

The Secret Series:

The Prelude of Ella and Micha

The Secret of Ella and Micha

The Forever of Ella and Micha

The Temptation of Lila and Ethan

The Ever After of Ella and Micha

Lila and Ethan: Forever and Always

Ella and Micha: Infinitely and Always

The Secret Star Grove Mysteries:

Ella & the Interrupted Road Trip

Ella & the Welcome Home

Untitled (coming soon)

Breaking Nova Series:

Breaking Nova

Saving Quinton

Delilah: The Making of Red

Nova and Quinton: No Regrets

Tristan: Finding Hope

Wreck Me

Ruin me

Unbeautiful Series:

Unbeautiful

Untamed

Tangled Realms:

Forever Violet

Untitled (coming soon)

Harlynn's Mystery Investigations:

Sugar Cookies & Zombie Secrets

Untitled (coming soon)

Mystic Willow Bay Vampires

Tempting Raven

Enchanting Raven

Alluring Raven

Untitled (coming soon)

Mystic Willow Bay Mysteries Series:

The Secret Life of a Witch

Broken Magic

Stolen Kisses

One Wild, Crazy, Zombie Night

Magical Whispers & the Undead

Untitled (coming soon)

Enchanted Chaos Series:

Enchanted Chaos

Shimmering Chaos

Iridescent Chaos (coming soon)

Capturing Magic:

The Thief of Wishes

The Thief of Magic

Untitled (coming soon)

My Cursed Superhero Life:

Grim

Untitled (coming soon)

Guardian Academy Series:

Entranced

Entangled

Enchanted

Entice

Charmed

Untitled (coming soon)

Monster Academy for the Magical:

Monster Academy for the Magical

Monster Academy for the Magical: Hidden Magic

Monster Academy for the Magical: The Monster Trial

Untitled (coming soon)

The Shattered Promises Series:

Shattered Promises

Fractured Souls

Unbroken

Broken Visions

Scattered Ashes

The Fallen Star Series:

The Fallen Star

The Underworld

The Vision

The Promise

The Lost Soul

The Evanescence

The Mist of Stars (untitled)

The Darkness Falls Series:

Darkness Falls

Darkness Breaks

Darkness Fades

The Death Collectors Series (NA and YA):

Ember X and Ember

Cinder X and Cinder

Spark X and Spark

Standalones:

The Forgotten Girl

www.ingramcontent.com/pod-product-compliance
Lightning Source LLC
Chambersburg PA
CBHW032144170626
46808CB00006B/2358